BLOOD HUNTERS

Steve Voake grew up in Midsomer Norton, near Bath. Before becoming a full-time writer, Steve was head teacher of a village school in Somerset. He is the critically acclaimed author of *The Dreamwalker's Child*, *The Web of Fire* and *The Starlight Conspiracy*. He lives with his family in Somerset.

BLOOD HUNTERS

STEVE VOAKE

faber and faber

First published in 2009
by Faber and Faber Limited
Bloomsbury House, 74–77 Great Russell Street, London
WCIB 3DA

Typeset by Faber and Faber Limited
Printed in England by CPI Bookmarque, Croydon

A CIP record for this book
is available from the British Library

ISBN 978–0–571–23001–3

4 6 8 10 9 7 5 3

BLOOD HUNTERS

The creatures moved in darkness.

They moved as they had done for millions of years, unseen and relentless, searching for signs of change.

Far above, in a world of sunlight and shadow, glaciers slid from mountains and melted into silver lakes. Forests grew, died and were replenished.

Such changes were barely detectable. They were of no more consequence than the flicker of starlight from a distant sun.

But this was something new.

The creatures gathered now, sensing strange tremors in the waters above. Their knowledge was instinctive; imprinted in every cell.

They are coming, it said.

Seek them out.

Seek them out . . .

'Hey, McDonald,' Crebbin called across the class-room, holding up his fist. 'I've got a present for you. Special delivery.'

Joe McDonald watched the shaven-headed Crebbin roll up his sleeves and knew the world was going to hurt him again, just the way it always did. But as he swallowed and stared at the floor the new boy, Giles Barclay, stepped forward and said, 'He didn't mean to do it. It was an accident, that's all.'

'Oh yeah?' Joe heard the anger in Crebbin's voice and was relieved to find that it was no longer directed at him.

'Well, maybe if you don't shut your mouth you'll have an accident too.'

Giles shrugged. 'Maybe I will,' he said. 'Let's find out, shall we?' He walked across to the open win-dow and sat on the ledge with his legs dangling into space.

'Meet you by the bike sheds.'

'You're crazy,' said Crebbin, suddenly nervous. 'You'll kill yourself.'

Joe peered down at the roof of the bike sheds. They were two floors up and it had to be a drop of at least five metres.

'Oh, I don't think so,' said Giles. 'But if I do, you can have my trainers.'

He winked at Joe.

Then he waved and jumped off the window ledge.

The problem had been caused, half an hour earlier, by a wasp.

They were in the science lab and Joe had been warning Giles about Crebbin.

'You want to be careful,' he told him. 'Not being funny or anything, but with your posh accent, you stand out a mile.'

But Giles had just smiled and said, 'I like standing out a mile. It's what I do.'

The wasp had begun buzzing around Joe's head and with a flick of the wrist, he'd sent it zinging across the desk where it cracked against Crebbin's forehead and ricocheted off into the window.

'Pang!' said Giles. 'Back of the net. Thank you and goodnight.'

But Crebbin had squeezed his knuckles and

stared at Joe angrily. 'I'll get you for that,' he hissed.

Wiping sweat from his forehead, Joe had watched Preston, the biology teacher, write 'threats to bio-diversity' on the board.

'His armpits for one,' Giles whispered, staring at the wet patches on the teacher's shirt. 'Toxic waste.'

'So, let's see who's done their homework,' Preston said. 'Who can tell me what is the biggest threat to the variety of life on our planet?'

On any other day, Joe would have stayed quiet. He knew it was better that way, staying on the fringes, not drawing attention to himself. But suddenly, sitting next to Giles, he had felt light-headed and reckless.

I like standing out a mile. It's what I do.

He put his hand up.

'Mr McDonald?'

'The biggest threat to the variety of life,' he said, 'is the human exploitation of the environment.'

'Alright,' said Preston, surprised by this. 'Good. And why is that?'

'We use huge amounts of natural resources and create vast amounts of waste. By 2050 there will be half as many of us again. So the size of the human population will cause irreparable damage to the environment.'

Preston was impressed. Shocked, even.

'What about growth-limiting factors?' he asked, trying to figure out whether this was just a fluke. 'What part do they play?'

Joe had seen Crebbin squeezing his knuckles. But he'd also seen Giles's smile growing wider by the second.

'In every eco-system,' he went on, remembering what his father had told him, 'all plants and animals have growth-limiting factors. Things which stop their numbers from becoming too big. If we don't limit our own growth, perhaps the earth will find a way of doing it for us.'

Afterwards, Giles had grinned and said, 'Very impressive, Professor. Where did you learn all that stuff?'

Joe had reddened. 'My dad teaches biology at the university. He talks about that kind of thing a lot.'

Now, shrieking with excitement, everyone clattered down the stairwell towards the bike sheds. By the time Joe got there, Crebbin was already squaring up to Giles, who was back on his feet and seemingly unhurt. He had landed feet first on the thin wooden roof of the sheds, crashing through it in a splinter of plywood.

'OK, new boy,' said Crebbin, beckoning Giles towards him with the tips of his fingers. 'Come and get it.'

Giles put down a piece of wood that he had been trying to fit back into the shed roof. Then he held up his hands and stepped backwards.

'Are you sure you want to do this?' he asked.

'Yeah,' said Crebbin. 'I'm sure.'

He stepped forward and swung a punch at Giles's head, but Giles quickly ducked beneath it and replied with a right hand that was so fast and hard it left Crebbin sitting on the ground, trying to stem the flow of blood from a bleeding nose.

A gasp of surprise went up from the crowd of onlookers.

Giles stepped back, waiting to see if Crebbin would get up again. But the punch had been a hard one, and Crebbin stayed put. Joe noticed that Giles appeared to be more concerned than angry, as though Crebbin were a small child who had fallen over. After a few moments he held out his hand and pulled Crebbin to his feet. Then he bent down and picked up a piece of broken plywood.

'I don't suppose,' he said, 'you'd give me a hand with this?'

As Joe watched Giles and Crebbin push the wood back into the broken roof he realised that – once again – life had taken an unexpected turn.

The world, it seemed, was full of surprises.

2

Three thousand miles away in the middle of the Mexican jungle, Professor William Sims was about to get a few surprises of his own. As he watched the project team lower the unmanned submarine DepthX (DEep Phreatic THermal eXplorer) into the water, he took out his camera phone and captured an image of the strange pumpkin-shaped object that dangled precariously in front of him.

'What do you think of her then, Professor? She's quite something, ain't she?'

Sims turned to look at the short, middle-aged man standing next to him and smiled. It was Dave Moreton, a well-respected professor of geology from the University of Texas. Enthusiasm sparkled in his eyes, and it was catching.

'Yes,' he agreed, his smile growing wider. 'She really is. Quite something.'

They stood together in the fierce heat and

watched the sub being lowered into El Zacatón, the world's deepest unexplored natural sinkhole.

As the waters closed over the top of the orange capsule and its outline faded away into the depths of the underwater cave, William Sims looked up through the circle of trees and thought how incredible life could be if you made the right choices.

Unfortunately for him, he was only hours away from making the wrong one.

'Come on in, William. We're just starting to get the first pictures.'

As he ducked inside the tent, Sims saw that the rest of the team was already gathered around the green glow of a computer screen. There were eleven of them: a couple from NASA, three from the Robotics Institute, three from Stone Aerospace and two professors from the University of Texas.

The smell of warm canvas combined with the heat and humidity to make Sims feel slightly queasy, but his excitement outweighed any feelings of discomfort.

He joined the others and saw that the blue water on the screen was becoming darker and murkier as the sub descended.

Two hours later the novelty of staring at small particles floating around underwater was starting to wear off when Jim Richler, the leader of the team from Stone Aerospace, made an announcement.

'OK, everyone, this is it, this is touchdown. We're currently at a depth of one thousand, two hundred and twenty-seven feet and we're about to reach the floor of the sinkhole. Gentlemen, we are now officially in unexplored territory. We have reached the bottom of the deepest known sinkhole on earth.'

There was a spontaneous burst of applause as everyone realised what had just been achieved.

'Incredible,' said Professor Moreton, smiling happily. 'Good work, guys!'

But then, as quickly as it had appeared, the smile vanished from his face. Sims turned back to look at the screen and felt the hairs on his neck prickle. Dark shapes swam towards them out of the blackness, wriggling and twisting in the glare of the submarine's spotlights.

'Hey,' whispered Moreton. 'What the hell are those things?'

'I don't know,' said Richler, his voice unusually quiet. 'I have no idea.'

For a few moments the only sound was the whir of the computer's cooling fan. Then, as the lights on the sub went out one by one and the screen was plunged into darkness, Richler swore and turned to the Aerospace guys who were already frantically tapping on their keyboards.

'Bring her up,' he told them, and Sims could hear the urgency in his voice. 'Bring her up now!'

When the sub surfaced just over an hour later, the sun was already sinking behind the trees and the light was fading fast. Sims watched the mobile crane winch it into the air and swing it toward the shore, water sluicing down the sides and pattering across the leaden surface of the sinkhole.

Moreton began to walk over, keen to get a first look, but Richler stopped him.

'Hang on, Professor,' he called. 'Wait until she's down.'

Moreton checked himself and smiled, embarrassed at his own enthusiasm.

'Hey, Harry!' called Richler, signalling to the crane driver as he lowered the sub onto the bank. 'Switch on the lights, will ya?'

The driver flipped a switch in his cab, activating a pair of headlamps on the front of the crane. Immediately the area around the sub was bathed in light.

Sims saw Moreton look at Richler, like a schoolboy checking to see if he was allowed to go and play.

Richler nodded and began walking towards the sub. 'OK,' he said. 'Let's take a look.'

* * *

The results were both disappointing and puzzling.

Disappointing, because there was no sign of the strange objects they had seen over a thousand feet beneath the surface.

Puzzling, because there was no damage to either the lights or the cameras.

'I don't get it,' said Richler, running his hands over the smooth metal skin of the sub. 'One minute they're covering the thing, the next minute they've completely disappeared. What're you thinking, John?'

The NASA guy stared at the sub for a moment and then switched his gaze to Richler. 'I'm thinking,' he said, 'that it sure beats the hell out of me.'

'I don't know about you guys,' said Richler, 'but it's dark and I need a drink. What do you say we head back to the lodge and check this thing over first thing in the morning?'

There were general murmurs of agreement, but as Sims bent down to pick up his bag he saw something move at the base of the sub. He turned to see if anyone else had noticed, but they were already halfway towards the vehicles, looking forward to a drink in the cool of the lodge. Kneeling down on the warm earth, he watched in wonder as a green, jelly-like substance oozed from the tiny gap between earth and metal, wriggling its way across the surface of the sub towards him.

He was about to shout for the others to come back and see his discovery when something stopped him. Perhaps it was the worry, somewhere at the back of his mind, that the others might take it away from him. Perhaps it was the thought that, finally, his chance had come to make his mark on the world. But whatever the reason, William Sims took a spatula and a small plastic specimen jar from his pocket, unscrewed the lid and flicked the squirming object into it. For a few moments he watched, fascinated, as the strange creature flowed across the bottom and then up the sides, as if searching for a way out.

'Hey, William!' called the voice of Professor Moreton in the darkness. 'Are you staying all night?'

Sims stood up in the gathering darkness and looked out across the black waters of El Zacatón. He would leave early tomorrow, he decided; make his excuses and fly back to the UK first thing in the morning.

'I'll be right with you,' he called.

Then, slipping the jar carefully into his pocket, he walked back towards the others.

3

The sun burned fiercely in a blue sky, white-hot and relentless. Streets surrendered to the blaze of heat and houses flung open their doors and windows, gasping for air.

Joe was still thinking about the way Giles had leapt out of that window and saved him from Crebbin.

Whoever would have thought of that as a solution?

His dad opened the refrigerator and pulled out a can of Coke, so cold that beads of moisture ran down the sides and dripped onto the kitchen floor.

'Like one?'

Joe held up a hand like a catcher on shortstop and the can thudded into his palm. He rolled it against his forehead, cold metal caressing his skin.

'Sorry I was late home last night. Things are busy at the university at the moment. You know how it is.'

Joe nodded. It was two years since his mother had died, and things were always busy at the university now.

'Any plans for today?'

Joe opened his Coke and took a sip.

'I might go over and see Giles later.'

'Who's Giles?'

'He's a new boy, just moved in. Got a treehouse and everything.'

Joe's dad closed his briefcase and looked at his watch; he was already thinking about going to work.

'A treehouse, eh? Well, listen, I've got a few things to sort out, but I'll be back around six.'

'But it's Saturday. How come you're going in today?'

Joe's dad smiled awkwardly. 'I had a bit of a disagreement with Bill yesterday.'

'What about?'

'Oh, it was nothing really. Storm in a teacup. But I want to try and smooth things over if I can. Make things better.'

He was quiet for a moment and Joe saw that he was staring at the fridge door, at the tattered old photograph of Joe and his mum running towards the waves with surfboards under their arms. But then he caught sight of Joe's reflection in the window and turned away.

'Well, I guess I should get going,' he said.

Joe nodded.

'I guess so,' he said.

At the end of the street, a blue Ford made a left turn, driving along the row of terraced houses until it reached number 26. The driver shifted into neutral, drifting the car into the kerb and turning off the engine. The hiss of air-conditioning dissolved into silence.

The men got out, squinting in the bright sunshine, the tarmac hot and sticky beneath their feet.

They moved to the pavement, checking the address once more before opening the gate.

Joe heard the doorbell, walked down the hallway and opened the front door.

There were two men, one mid-thirties, the other older.

The older one asked, 'Does Martin McDonald live here?'

But before Joe could answer, his dad arrived and Joe stepped back to let him pass.

'That's me. How can I help you?'

The older man opened his wallet and showed him a badge. Then he took a piece of paper from his pocket and held it in the space between them.

'Martin McDonald,' he said, 'I am arresting you on suspicion of the murder of William Sims.'

4

The body of William Sims lay untidily where it had fallen, like a bundle of clothes thrown carelessly to the floor. One hand stretched out beneath the worktops, reaching towards the pen that was gathering dust next to a forgotten paperclip. A dark pool of blood stained the front of his white shirt.

'Take some over here when you're done with that.' Detective Sergeant Harris was crouching on the floor, peering at something.

'What is it?'

'See for yourself.'

The photographer squeezed off a few more shots, then crouched next to Harris and stared at the broken glass that lay scattered beneath the worktop. There was a puddle of water, and at the edge of the puddle nearest to Sims's body the water was tinged with crimson.

'Fish tank?' suggested the photographer, standing

up and pressing the camera to his eye once more.

'Maybe,' said Harris. 'But where are the fish?'

The photographer held the shutter for three clicks before lowering the camera again. One of the neon tube lights was flickering and the blinds were still drawn. A half-drunk cup of coffee stood on the worktop next to a pad of paper.

'Have you seen this?' he asked, looking at the pad.

Harris stood up, stretched, put his hands in the small of his back.

'Yeah,' he said. 'I've seen it.'

The photographer zoomed in on the words.

Rapid growth rate. High mobility. Intelligent.

'What's it mean?'

'I have no idea,' said Harris, stepping back from the puddle and flapping his shirt to create a breeze. It was 30 degrees and there was no air-conditioning. 'But the uniform boys have pulled in a colleague of his – one Martin McDonald. Maybe he can enlighten us.'

The photographer moved carefully around the room the way he had been trained, anxious not to step on anything that might affect the crime scene.

'Come and look at this,' said Harris, pointing at

the floor.

Together they stared at the trail of water, so thin it was barely visible. Then they followed it across the room until they reached the small washroom, where the trail led all the way to the base of the toilet. A faint line of moisture glistened across the porcelain and on the wooden seat there were three specks of blood.

'What is that?' asked Harris, crouching down as the photographer pressed the shutter. 'What the *hell* is that?'

5

'There must be some mistake,' said Joe as the young policeman pushed his father gently but firmly into the back seat of the police car. 'He didn't do anything.'

'Don't worry,' said his father. He tried to disguise the fear in his voice but Joe could feel its sharp edges like stones beneath sand. 'We'll soon have this sorted out. I'll be home by the end of the day.'

The policeman looked at Joe.

'Is there someone who can look after you for the time being?'

Joe saw that he didn't really care, that this was simply a procedure he needed to follow.

'My mum's out,' he said quietly as they slammed the car door. 'I'll tell her when she gets back.'

He watched the car until it disappeared around the corner. Then he went back into the house, took the front-door key off the hook and went out again, closing the door behind him.

When he reached the street, he started to run.

On summer evenings the towpath was alive with people: joggers, couples strolling and cyclists steering a careful path between them. But now it was mid-day, and the towpath was deserted. Tall grasses mixed with dark green nettles below a froth of cow parsley. Bees buzzed from comfrey to campion, jostling with foxgloves for the space in between. On the far side, the canal reflected the willows that grew on the bank, dipping their branches into its quiet waters.

Joe had been running for ten minutes; his mouth was dry and his spit as thick as tree sap. When he reached the bridge, he leaned on the wooden rail and paused for breath. On the other side of the canal he could see a large Edwardian house, partially hidden by leaves.

Mine's the one with the treehouse. Come over any time.

There was a path leading to a small gate and a woodland garden. Through a curtain of green leaves he could see a rope ladder hanging below a pale blue den that nestled in the branches, five metres above the ground.

Giles sat with his feet dangling over the edge and his

head resting on the branch above, reading a book. As Joe approached, a twig snapped beneath his feet and Giles looked up and smiled.

'Hey,' he called, closing his book. 'Come on up.'

When he reached the top of the ladder, Joe followed Giles through the doorway and they sat on a couple of the brightly coloured cushions that were scattered around the floor. It was cooler inside, but not much. In the middle was a low table with some sweet wrappers, a flask and a small pile of paperbacks on it. At the far end, through the open window, Joe could see a path leading through the trees to the back of the house.

'You alright?' asked Giles. 'You look knackered.'

'I've been running,' said Joe. 'My dad's been arrested.'

Giles raised his eyebrows.

'Say again?'

'They took him away about half an hour ago.'

'Seriously?'

'Uh-huh.'

'Whatever for?'

Joe shook his head, hardly able to bring himself to say the words.

'Something to do with a murder.'

Giles whistled.

'Bit of a gangster, is he?'

'No. He's a lecturer at the university.'

'Oh, OK. Just asking.' Giles unscrewed the flask, poured some lemonade into a plastic cup and handed it to Joe. Small chunks of ice cracked and splintered, tiny icebergs in a yellow sea. Joe took a sip and imagined cool rain falling somewhere far away.

'Next question,' said Giles. 'Not being rude or anything, but what are you doing here?'

Joe shrugged.

'I don't know,' he said. 'You just seemed like the sort of person who might be able to help.'

Joe put his elbows on his knees and rested his forehead in the palms of his hands.

'I don't know what to do, Giles,' he said. 'I just don't know what to do.'

'Don't worry,' said Giles, putting down his glass and getting to his feet. 'Not knowing what to do is always a good place to start.'

6

Martin McDonald sat with his hands resting on the table, wondering what would happen next. The room was sparse: white walls, a single table and two chairs facing one another. High up in the corner was a video camera, fixed to a steel bracket. The room was functional. It said: we don't know if you are guilty or not, but this is the place where we will find out.

He thought of Joe and hoped he would sit tight for a couple of hours until this got sorted out. But for now the world consisted only of this white cell, a nowhere room with a table, chairs, four walls and a ceiling.

The door opened and a man in his mid-fifties walked in, placing a tape recorder on the table between them.

'Are we doing this to music?' Martin asked, making a joke, although his heart was not in it.

The man looked at him, but didn't smile. 'Just standard procedure, Mr McDonald,' he said. 'Just our way of making sure we've all said the things we think we said.'

'This is crazy,' said Martin. 'You know that, right? Bill was my friend.'

'Mr McDonald, my name is Detective Sergeant Harris. I am quite sure you have already been told this, but it is my duty to remind you that you do not have to say anything, but it may harm your defence if you do not mention when questioned something that you later rely on in court. Anything you do say may be given in evidence.'

Martin watched Harris push the record and play buttons, heard the click and whir of the tape, knew that from now on, whatever he said could never be taken back or denied.

'The time is 11.32 on Saturday, 26th July. This is the first formal interview with Martin McDonald who has been arrested on suspicion of the murder of William Sims on the night of Friday, 25th July.'

Martin shook his head.

'I want a solicitor,' he said. 'I'm not answering any questions without a solicitor present.'

Harris nodded, as if he had been expecting this.

'Do you have a solicitor?' he asked.

'No,' said Martin, who neither had nor knew how

to get one. 'What should I do?'

'We can arrange that for you,' said Harris, trying to be professional about it. But Martin could see he was irritated, that he had wanted to get this over with and now he would have to wait.

Harris stopped the tape, got up and walked to the door.

'Can I get you anything else? Cigarettes? A cup of coffee?'

Martin shook his head.

'Just a glass of water, please.'

'A glass of water it is.'

Harris closed the door and suddenly Martin was alone again, staring at the white walls and wondering how long this would take.

Hours.

Days.

Maybe a lifetime.

7

Trevor Wilkins had always believed he would make his fortune by the time he was forty.

When he was eighteen, he told everyone he was going to start his own business, make a few million and retire while he was young enough to enjoy it. He dreamed of fast cars, lavish parties and a mansion with a swimming pool and a hot tub.

Unfortunately for Trevor, these dreams didn't match up with reality. In the late 1980s he went into property development just as the housing market collapsed and he lost all his money.

So instead of becoming a millionaire, he became a plumber.

Which was why, at forty-five years old, he was not sitting on a yacht in the south of France, watching the sun go down and listening to the clink of ice in his gin and tonic.

Instead he was sitting in a white van with the

words *Wilkins Plumbing & Heating Services* written on the side in big red letters.

But Trevor had never lost sight of his dream. He knew that there were still plenty of stupid people out there, ready to give him lots of money in return for sorting out their problems. For most people, plumbing was a mysterious art that they did not understand. They neither knew what Trevor did nor how much it cost. So although they were often shocked by the size of the bill, there wasn't a whole lot they could do about it.

Old people were the best. Trevor could charge them a couple of hundred quid just for changing a washer on a tap. He would just tell them there were problems with the boiler and spend an hour or two drinking their tea and banging about in the airing cupboard with a spanner. They would shake their heads and say, *Well it seems like an awful lot of money*.

But they always coughed up in the end.

So every day, his bank balance got a little bit bigger. It was still some way short of a million, but a few more years of leaky pipes, dripping taps and burned-out boilers and Trevor knew he'd be dipping his toes in the Med, sipping on an ice-cold beer.

'Hello,' he said, all friendly like, as the front door opened to reveal an old man dressed in brown slacks and a grey cardigan. 'I've come about the drains.'

'Oh, thank goodness.' The old man's expression changed to one of relief. 'Come on through.'

Trevor followed him down the narrow hallway and together they stood at the back door, staring at a backyard swimming in five centimetres of filthy, stinking water. On the top was a brown scum, made up of vegetable peelings, pieces of soggy tissue paper and other things that Trevor didn't even want to think about. As the surface water evaporated in the heat, steam drifted into the air, strengthening the smell of rotting vegetables and sewage.

'It's probably a blockage,' said the old man.

'You think?'

Trevor was annoyed that life was still throwing this kind of stuff at him. Mentally he was already doubling the size of his bill. But then he remembered that it never pays to upset the customer, so he added, 'I think you're right. I just need to go and get some kit.'

Back at the van, he pulled on a pair of waterproof waders and some rubber gloves, then took out a set of drain rods.

'Do you reckon you can sort it out?' asked the old man as Trevor clumped back down the hallway.

'Let's find out, shall we?' said Trevor. He stepped out into the stinking sunshine and stared at the pool of water. There was a pipe coming from the back of the house which carried waste water from the sink and washing machine. He guessed that the blockage had to be some way along the drain, causing it to back up into the yard.

Wrinkling his nose against the smell, he stepped down and sloshed over to where the pipe disappeared beneath the water. Feeling around with his boot, he located the drain and wiggled his toes to see if there was any movement. He felt something soft, and decided that perhaps the job would be easier than he thought. Laying the rods on the steps for a moment, he bent down and pushed his hand into the water.

Again he felt something soft. He guessed vegetable peelings and solidified cooking oil; maybe a few other treats thrown into the mix. He gave a hard tug and the obstruction came away in his hand. Immediately the water began to swirl around him, rushing down into the drain with such unexpected force that it sucked his arm down with it, sending him splashing to his knees.

Swearing, he plunged his other hand beneath the water and used it to steady himself, trying to drag his arm out of the pipe. 'Hey!' he shouted, turning his head towards the old man. But the old man had wandered back inside to make a cup of tea and as he slipped around in the brown, slimy water, Trevor tried not to panic. He tried to remember that the water was not rising but falling, that soon the pressure would be off his hand and he would be able to remove it once more.

But as he waited, something bumped and squirmed against his fingers. Then a sharp, agonising pain carved through his wrist like a blade from a ripsaw.

'Aaaagh!' he screamed, pulling away even harder. Suddenly his arm was free and he was sitting back watching the water swirl down into the unblocked drain. He felt strangely weak, as if all his strength was washing away with the dirt and the debris. It was only then that he noticed the water around him had turned a dull shade of red. He looked down and saw that where his hand should have been there was now only a mess of torn, ragged flesh. And as the blood continued to leak away into the gurgling water, Trevor began to call, softly at first, then louder and louder.

'Help me! Someone! Help me, please!'

As he waited, he thought he saw something slither away beneath the surface of the water. But then he fell back against the steps, and as his eyelids began to flutter and close, he stared at the blue sky and imagined he was looking down upon an endless blue sea, where at last he could sail away from this ordinary life for ever.

8

'I don't understand,' said Joe as they climbed onto the bus. 'My father would never murder anyone. Not in a million years.'

'OK,' said Giles, watching Joe fumble in his pocket for change. 'So that's what we tell them.' He paid the bus driver and together they clambered up to the top deck.

'I'll pay you back,' Joe said as they took a seat at the front. 'I promise.'

'Tell you what,' said Giles, 'the next time one of my relatives gets arrested, you can pay the bus fare.'

As the bus ground its gears and lumbered down a narrow lane, Joe listened to the branches scratch against the window and thought about the way his father had looked at the photograph on the fridge door. They had been so happy back then, just the three of them beneath a blue sky. But now the clouds were gathering again. And as he leaned his forehead against the window he could feel the world closing in on him once more. 'Leave me alone,' he whispered, squeezing his eyes tight shut. 'Please. Just leave me alone.'

The desk sergeant looked surprised, as if he were used to seeing people by appointment only.

'Yes?' he said. 'Can I help you?'

'I hope so,' said Giles, striding up to the hatch. 'We're here about a case of mistaken identity.'

'Pardon me?' The desk sergeant raised an eyebrow and Joe decided it was time to get involved.

'You've got my dad here,' he said, 'and he hasn't done anything. So you need to let him go.'

'Oh,' said the sergeant, looking from one to the other. 'I see.' His eyes settled on Giles.

'And why are you here?'

'For moral support,' said Giles, looking him squarely in the eye.

The sergeant turned back to Joe.

'What's your name, son?'

'Joe,' said Joe. 'Joe McDonald.'

When the sergeant heard the surname, he nodded.

'We sent someone along to make sure you were OK, but you weren't there.'

'That's because he came to see me,' said Giles.

'Ah,' replied the sergeant, scratching the stubble on his chin. 'For moral support, I suppose.' He put down his pen, said, 'One moment,' and then disappeared through a door at the back.

As they waited, Joe looked around at the posters telling him not to drink and drive or leave his valuables in a car he hadn't got. Giles stared at a picture of a man in a white coat, holding up a sign which read *It pays to talk. Ring Crimestoppers: 0800 555 111.*

'Maybe we will,' he said. 'Maybe we'll ask for a refund.'

A door opened and a young policewoman walked in.

'Hello,' she said, looking at Joe. 'You must be Joe McDonald.'

Joe nodded. 'That's me.'

'Alright, Joe, well I would like to speak with you for a while, if that's OK.'

She glanced at Giles.

'Will you excuse us for a minute?'

'Do I have a choice?'

'No.'

'See you in a minute, then.'

The room had pale blue walls, comfortable chairs and a notice board crowded with pieces of paper. There was a sink in one corner with jars of coffee, teabags, cups and glasses. There was also a white-board on the wall with the date written on it in blue marker pen. Underneath it someone had written: 'All evaluations to me by tomorrow AT THE LAT-EST.'

For a moment, Joe felt strangely comforted. *There is order here*, he thought. *Perhaps these people will be able to help me.* But then he remembered the reason he was there and his feelings of hopelessness returned.

The policewoman was younger than the sergeant and appeared newer, less crumpled, as though she had only recently come off the production line. Her dark skirt had sharp creases and her white shirt was perfectly ironed. When she smiled, her teeth matched her shirt.

'My name's Susie,' she said, resting her hands in her lap like someone about to have their photo-graph taken. 'I'm from the Child Protection Team.'

Joe stared up at the neon light that was flickering on the ceiling.

'They think he murdered someone, don't they?'

'Not necessarily, Joe. But, OK, I'll be honest with you. A man called William Sims died at the univer-sity and your dad was there around the time it hap-pened. So because of that, the police need to ques-tion him.'

As she spoke, Joe felt a stab of shock as he remembered something his father had said that morning.

I had a bit of a disagreement with Bill yesterday.

'Are you alright?' Susie asked, a look of concern on her face. 'You've gone very pale.'

'I'm fine,' said Joe, trying to keep his expression neutral. 'I'm absolutely fine.'

But inside the questions were already forming:

Could he have done it?

Could my father be a murderer . . .?

It was 12.30 p.m.

Maureen Lewis stood in the bathroom and looked nervously at the toilet seat. She had used two rolls of Sellotape, wrapping them around the lid until it looked like some kind of weird parcel.

But she was still worried.

She put her fingers beneath the lid and pulled, testing it for movement. The seat moved a fraction, taking up the slack where the tape was not as tight as it could be.

'Oh no,' she whispered. 'That's no good at all.'

Backing out onto the landing, she walked along to the study and picked up her old sewing-machine case, a legacy from her mother. The case was heavier than she remembered, but that was a good thing.

The heavier the better.

She bent her knees and lifted, the way she had been taught at the tobacco factory before she retired. Forty years of lifting boxes of cigarette cartons might not have been everyone's idea of a life fulfilled, but at least it meant that, at seventy-eight years old, she still knew how to pick up a sewing machine.

Her bare feet padding across the carpet, she steered herself around the door and into the bathroom, dropping the heavy case onto the toilet lid with a thump. As she leaned on it to catch her breath, she heard a key turn in the lock downstairs and the creak of the front door opening.

'Mum? It's me, Lesley.'

Maureen suddenly felt very tired. She sat on the edge of the bath and slid down until she was sitting on the floor. Staring at a patch of toothpaste on the carpet, she wondered, absent-mindedly, why she hadn't noticed it before. Just recently, even the smallest things had become difficult.

Lesley stopped in the bathroom doorway and stared, first at her mother, then at the sewing machine and the taped-up toilet.

'Oh, *Mum*,' she said. 'Whatever have you been doing?'

Maureen shook her head and, when she spoke, her voice was thin and quiet.

'They're trying to get in,' she said. 'They're trying to get in and I don't want them in my house.'

She looked at her daughter with frightened eyes.

'You won't let them in, will you, Lesley? Please, say you won't let them in!'

'Sssh!' said Lesley, thinking how strange and sad this business of growing old was, the way it turned daughters into mothers and mothers back into daughters again.

'Come on. Let's get you into bed.'

Taking her mother gently by the arm, she helped her across the landing and into the bedroom. She turned back the blue candlewick bedspread and plumped up the pillows, smoothing out the bottom sheet with her palm.

'That's it,' she said as her mother rested her head against the quilted headboard. 'I'm going to ask Doctor Wells to call round and take a look at you. Now, what would you say to a nice cup of tea?'

Maureen closed her eyes, surrendering to tiredness at last. 'That would be lovely,' she whispered. 'You're such a good girl, Lesley.'

Lesley smiled.

'It was you who made me that way,' she said.

After taking the tea to her mother, Lesley returned the sewing machine to its proper place and was just pulling off the last of the Sellotape when the doorbell rang. Screwing the tape into a sticky ball, she hurried down the stairs and opened the door to find her mother's GP waiting on the step.

'Problems?' asked Doctor Wells by way of a greeting.

As Lesley explained, he scratched his beard and nodded sympathetically.

'These strange imaginings are not as uncommon as you might think,' he told her. 'I'm afraid her grip on reality may become weaker as her condition progresses.'

Lesley took him upstairs to where her mother lay with the bedclothes pulled up to her chin, although outside the sun was hot enough to wilt the flowers in the window box.

The doctor listened patiently as the old lady told him about the things that came in the night.

'The mind can play cruel tricks on us, Mrs Lewis,' he told her. 'But don't worry. I have something that will help to make the bad things go away.'

'Thank you, Doctor,' said Maureen, gratefully swallowing the pills with a little water. 'You're very kind.'

As they reached the front door, the doctor put a reassuring hand on Lesley's arm. 'I've given her some mild sedatives, that's all. Something to calm her nerves. Will you be able to keep an eye on her today?'

'Oh yes,' said Lesley. 'I have to go shopping, but I'll pop in again later.'

'Good. In that case, if she still seems anxious, give her another two pills, and then another two just before she goes to sleep. If there are any further problems, let me know.'

'Thank you, Doctor,' said Lesley. 'I really appreciate it. We both do.'

When she checked on her mother again, she was pleased to hear the deep, gentle sound of her breathing. She was asleep.

Lesley was halfway down the stairs when she imagined she heard a small, watery sound, like a fish caught in shallow water. She smiled, shook her head and thought, *Mum's not the only one imagining things.*

Then she opened the front door and closed it behind her.

It was a simple act, but one that saved her life without her even knowing it.

10

Even before the door opened, Joe could see his father through the square of glass. He was sitting at the table with his chin resting on his hands, staring into space. He looked pale and tired; older somehow. For a moment Joe just wanted to run and tell him that everything would be alright. But he knew from experience that the world was cunning, that it was out to hurt him. He knew that if he was going to figure this thing out, it was important to keep his distance.

He also knew that there was a question he had to ask.

Susie opened the door and Joe's dad looked up.

'Joe!' he said, as though he had found something precious that had been lost.

Joe walked slowly towards his father and hugged him, but not too tightly and not for too long.

'Are you OK?'

'I'm fine,' said Joe, stepping back. 'Giles said I can stay with him for a while.'

'Don't worry, Mr McDonald,' Susie reassured him. 'We're keeping an eye on things. We'll make sure that Joe's well looked after.'

'If you'd let me out of here,' said Joe's dad, 'I could save you the trouble.'

He looked at the uniformed police officer in the corner, then back at Susie again.

'I don't suppose you could give us a minute?'

Susie glanced uncertainly at the other officer.

'I don't know whether we . . .'

'Just two minutes, that's all. It's not a lot to ask, is it? I just want to talk to my son.'

Susie looked at the other officer again and he nodded.

'Five minutes, then. We'll be right outside.'

'Thank you. Thank you very much.'

Joe's dad waited until they left the room, then he hugged Joe again. 'Don't cry,' he said. 'It'll be alright.'

'I'm not crying,' said Joe, wiping his eyes with the back of his hand. Then he moved away and sat in the chair opposite. He stared at the table. 'Will you tell me the truth?' he asked, afraid to look up in case he saw something in his father's eyes he didn't want to see. 'Please?'

'What do you mean, Joe? The truth about what?'

Joe transferred his gaze to the white walls, saw tiny cracks that he hadn't noticed before.

'About what happened.'

For a few seconds a silence hung between them. Joe's heart beat so fast that he was sure his father would hear it.

'Are you asking me if I did it?'

Joe swallowed and took a breath, gulping as though he was coming up for air.

'Well, did you?'

Joe's dad reached across the table and closed a hand over Joe's tight, bunched fist.

'Joe, look at me.'

Slowly, Joe looked up, terrified of what he might see. But his father's eyes were calm and clear. And when he said, 'I didn't do it, Joe,' it was as if, somewhere beneath the crumbling earth, he had found something solid on which to stand.

'What can I do?' he asked. 'Tell me what I can do.'

'Alright. The first thing you have to do is trust me.'

'OK,' said Joe. His hands shook, but his father steadied them with his own.

'I need you to do something for me.'

Joe nodded.

'Anything. Just say it.'

Joe's father looked at the door, checking that no one was listening.

'I need you to phone someone. Professor Dave Moreton in Texas. His number's in my address book, on the desk in my study. When you get through to him, I want you to tell him what's happened, and then I want you to ask him one question: Did anything strange happen in Mexico last week?'

'Why?' Joe heard the sound of the door handle turning behind him. 'Do you think this has something to do with that?'

'I don't know. But I think it might.'

'OK,' said Joe as the police officer walked into the room.

'Everything alright?' asked Susie, walking in behind him.

'Everything's fine,' said Joe. He hugged his dad goodbye and told him that he would see him soon. But in his mind he was saying two words to himself, over and over, saying them so he wouldn't forget.

Dave Moreton, Dave Moreton . . .

11

Maureen Lewis was awake now, staring at the curtains. They were made from a simple cotton fabric and their print taken from an old-fashioned design, a floral motif of red poppies dancing across a base of light and dark greens. They reminded her of a summer picnic she had been on once with her husband Charlie. She had been dreaming about it. She had even imagined that she heard the splash of water over stones, of trout jumping for flies in the river.

'Charlie?' she whispered. 'Charlie, is that you?'

Her mind was playing tricks again. Of course it wasn't Charlie. He'd been dead for over twenty years. The doctor had warned her that the tablets were strong. Her eyelids began to close and her limbs felt heavy, almost as though they belonged to someone else.

Perhaps she should just give in to it.

Get some rest.

Suddenly her eyelids fluttered open again. Had she heard something? Or was she just imagining it? Slowly she pulled herself up into a sitting position and tried to concentrate.

It was then that she remembered the strange noises she had heard in the bathroom late at night. *That* was why she had taped the toilet lid shut and put the sewing machine on top.

It had made her feel safer.

But then Lesley had come round and made a great song and dance about things, the way she always did. She had called Doctor Wells and he had given her pills to make her sleep. But neither of them had heard the things Maureen had heard.

Suddenly a thought occurred to her.

If Lesley thinks I'm going mad, she won't know. She'll have moved it . . .

Fear seeped into her veins. How long had she been asleep?

She had to act now.

Before it came back.

Splaying her hands flat on the mattress, Maureen moved one leg to the side of the bed and slid it down onto the floor. Then she did the same with the other leg, moving herself around until she was sitting on the edge of the bed. The effort required for this simple manoeuvre was so great that she was tempted just to lie down again. But fear cut through her exhaustion, pushing her unsteadily to her feet. She staggered across the bedroom and rested her head against the wall, feeling her eyes start to close once more.

'Come on, Maureen,' she told herself. 'You have to do this. You *have* to.'

Stumbling across the bedroom carpet, she tottered across the landing and stood unsteadily in the bathroom doorway, swaying like a sapling in a breeze.

'Oh no,' she whispered, holding on to the door frame and staring at the open toilet lid. 'Oh no.'

Narrowing her eyes against the sunlight that streamed through the bathroom window, she put her head on one side and listened, fearful of what she might hear. But there was nothing except her own shallow breathing and the ticking of the grand-father clock.

Maybe it wasn't here yet.

Maybe there was still time.

Using the banister rail for support, she edged her way back along the landing until she reached the spare room where, as she had suspected, Lesley had returned the sewing machine to its original position on top of the table.

'Oh, Lesley,' she whispered. 'Why can't you leave things alone?'

Putting her hands beneath the sewing machine, she tried to lift it the way she had done before, but it seemed much heavier since her last attempt.

'Come on,' she told herself. 'Come on!'

She bent forward and rested her forehead on the top of the sewing machine's wooden case. Then, gritting her teeth and screwing her eyes tightly shut, she pulled with all her strength and lifted the sewing machine off the table. Wheezing under the strain, she turned and wobbled back towards the doorway, bumping against the wall as she went. She could see sunlight now, shining through the bathroom door. Suddenly all that mattered was to carry the sewing machine, carry the sewing machine – she repeated it with each lurching step – carry the sewing machine and the bad things won't come and everything will be alright . . .

Without warning, the sewing machine slipped from her grasp and crashed heavily to the floor. At the same moment Maureen's legs buckled beneath her and she fell next to it with a cry of frustration.

'Damn it!' she cried angrily, summoning up the worst swear word she could think of. 'Damn it, damn it, damn it!'

She tried to stand but she felt washed out,

exhausted, desperate for sleep.

'No,' she told herself. 'I can do this. I can do it.'

Forcing herself to her knees, she placed both hands on the smooth wood of the sewing machine case and pushed.

The sewing machine slid forward.

'Right,' she said.

She pushed again and it slid a little further.

'Yes!' she said. 'Come on, Maureen.'

Three minutes later she was sitting on the bathroom floor next to the toilet with her head resting on the top of the sewing machine. Stretching out her hand, she slammed the toilet lid down.

'OK, Maureen,' she said. 'Last bit, girl.'

Pushing herself up onto her knees, she slid her fingers beneath the base of the sewing machine and pulled it against her chest, toppling forward onto the toilet lid with a crash. Then she sat back on her haunches and wiped the sweat from her forehead. The sewing machine was firmly on top of the toilet seat.

Safe at last.

With a sigh of relief, she put her hand on the towel rail and pulled herself to her feet. Stumbling back into the darkness of the bedroom she gazed at the patterned flowers on the curtains and thought, *Charlie would have been proud of me.*

But as she closed the door and pulled back the duvet, she heard the sound again.

Something moving across the carpet.

'Who's there?' she called in a small, frightened voice. 'Who is it? I'll call the police!'

She caught a glimpse of something then, something in the shadows beside the wardrobe.

'Oh no,' she whispered faintly, reaching for the curtains, desperate for the light. 'Help me, Charlie! Help me, please!'

But as her hand clutched at the edge of the curtain, the darkness uncoiled itself and sprang at her, tearing at her throat with such violence that her screams dissolved into the redness of poppies and then Charlie was calling to her and all the colours and sounds became nothing but the bright and endless hiss of light.

12

The policeman on duty at Joe's house was young and inexperienced. He had been on training courses and read all the handbooks, but nothing had taught him how to deal with a thirteen-year-old boy who wanted to go up to his bedroom.

'I'm afraid I can't let you in right now,' he said, looking over his shoulder and hoping that one of his more experienced colleagues would appear. 'It's a crime scene.'

'No it isn't,' said Joe. 'It's my house.'

'Like I said: it's a crime scene.'

'Are you sure you've got your facts right?' asked Giles. 'I mean, it's not really a crime scene, is it? The crime scene is over at the university. This is just a place which they think might be *connected* to a crime. So technically it's not a crime scene at all. I expect you've just got confused. I think what we're dealing with here is a search warrant, which isn't the same thing at all.'

Joe saw that the young policeman was confused. He hadn't been expecting this, and wasn't sure how to respond. But they had told him not to let anyone in, and he was sticking to it.

Giles made a point of peering past him down the hallway.

'Is there someone else we can talk to?' he asked. 'Someone in authority?'

The young policeman sighed. He took his cap off and wiped his forehead with his sleeve.

'Wait there,' he said. 'I'll see what the situation is inside.'

Joe turned to Giles and raised his eyebrows. 'Where did you learn that stuff about search warrants? The Discovery Channel?'

Giles smiled. 'While you were off chatting to your lady friend, I was talking to the sergeant on reception. Reckon he must get bored, sitting there on his own all day. He was very helpful, actually. Told me all kinds of things.' His smile grew wider. 'Don't think he got much work done though.'

'Giles,' Joe asked, 'do you really think we can do this? Do you think we can make everything right again?'

'Yeah, why not?' said Giles. 'The way I see it, when life bowls you a fast one you've just got to step up and smack it into the stands.'

'But I'm no good at cricket,' said Joe.

Giles looked at him sideways. 'In that case,' he said, 'you'd better start practising.'

The young policeman returned with an older man who wore a blue shirt with a patterned tie. The man was in his fifties with thinning hair. His eyes had lost their shine, perhaps because of age or, perhaps, because of the things that they had seen.

'Problem?' he asked, leaning on the door frame.

'I live here,' said Joe, 'and I want to come in.'

The man considered this for a moment.

'What's your name, son?'

'Joe McDonald.'

'OK.' He turned to Giles. 'And how about you?'

'Giles,' said Giles.

'Any relation?'

'Just a friend.'

The man nodded, weighing up the situation. Then he turned back to Joe.

'Has anyone from the Children's Team seen you yet?'

'I met someone called Susie,' Joe told him. 'I'm staying with Giles and she said I could pick up some things.'

For the moment, the man seemed satisfied with

this answer.

'Alright,' he said. 'I guess you'd better come on through.' As they walked down the hallway Joe heard voices upstairs; strangers in his house.

They sat in the lounge, Joe and Giles side by side on the blue sofa, the policeman in the easy chair in the corner.

'I'm Detective Sergeant Harris,' he said. 'I know this must be difficult for you, but as soon as we're done we'll be out of your way, OK?'

Joe nodded. His expression was blank but his mind was racing.

'Is it alright if I go and get my stuff?' he asked.

'Is it in your bedroom?'

'Yes.'

Harris studied him, professionally suspicious for a moment. Then he seemed to relax.

'Sure, go ahead. But don't touch anything else, OK?'

As Joe climbed the stairs he heard Giles ask, 'What's it like being a police officer? It must be very interesting.' He heard the low rumble of Harris's reply and realised that Giles was trying to buy him some time. But he guessed Harris wasn't stupid and that he didn't have much time.

There were two men in his father's bedroom, their backs to the door. The drawers had been removed from the bedside table and their contents stacked in neat piles on the bed. Next to them were several plastic bags filled with seemingly random objects: a pen, some socks from the wash basket, a nail file.

Joe kept on moving, peering into his own bedroom which appeared to have been left untouched. His books and pencils were still arranged neatly on the desk, just as he'd left them. The next room along was the room his father used as a study. Joe often heard him tapping away on the keyboard late at night, writing up some important paper or notes for the next day's lectures.

His number's in my address book, on the desk in my study.

Joe tiptoed into the room and saw that the men had been here too. There were more plastic bags arranged in little rows along one wall: inside them were papers, files and snippets of information that the police were obviously hoping would prove his father's guilt.

Dave Moreton, he reminded himself. *Dave Moreton, address book, on the desk . . .*

But when he looked, there was no address book. The surface of the desk was clear.

He crouched down for a closer look at the bags and saw that one contained several notebooks. At the bottom was another, smaller book.

Joe could hear the men talking in the next room. He glanced at the clock on the wall and realised he had already been gone for several minutes.

He had to act now.

The bag had 'Police Evidence Bag' printed on it and a red seal at the top. But no one had sealed it yet. The bag was still open.

Carefully, he removed the notebooks one by one. At the bottom was the address book. His hand shaking, he removed it and turned to the *M* section. He ran his finger down through the lines: Maggs, McDonald, McDonald, Moreton.

Professor David Moreton. (512-471-3160).

Joe whispered the number to himself: '512-471-3–'

'Hey!'

Joe jumped and snapped the book shut.

'What are you doing?'

Joe turned to see that Harris was standing in the doorway with his hands in his pockets.

He didn't look happy.

13

'I asked you what you were doing.'

'Nothing. I wasn't doing anything.'

'Don't lie to me, son. I don't like it when people lie to me.'

Joe swallowed and tried to keep calm, but it wasn't easy with Harris glaring at him from the doorway.

'I'm not lying. I was just . . . looking through some of my dad's stuff, that's all.'

'Stuff that's in a bag marked "Police Evidence"?'

'Sorry. I wasn't thinking.'

'You weren't thinking, huh?'

Joe glanced quickly at Harris and saw that he wasn't buying it.

'Is that the same kind of not thinking as the kind where you tell me you're coming upstairs to get your stuff and then just, sort of, go into the wrong room?'

Not waiting for an answer, Harris strode across

the room and took the address book from Joe's hand.

'What were you looking for, eh? What were you trying to find?'

Joe saw that Harris had the address book open at the page he had been looking at. And although he had no idea why his father wanted him to call Moreton, something told him it was better if Harris didn't know about it.

'I was looking for my uncle's number,' he said, suddenly inspired.

'Your uncle?'

'Yes.' Joe pointed at the page. 'Third one down, see? Richard McDonald. I just wanted to talk to him.'

Harris regarded him suspiciously.

'About what?'

Joe shrugged and looked around.

'About all of this.'

He hardly knew his uncle, of course, saw him once a year at Christmas, but – for the moment at least – Harris seemed to accept his answer. Sensing an opportunity, Joe held out his hand.

'Can I have it back?' he asked. 'So I can write down the number?'

But Harris wasn't stupid. He took a pen from his top pocket, scribbled something on a piece of paper and held it out between finger and thumb.

'There,' he said. 'There's your number.'

Then he took the address book, dropped it into the bag and placed the other books on top of it. He looked at Joe expectantly.

'So. Are you going to phone him?'

'Maybe later.'

Joe could see from Harris's expression that he would be paying special attention to the address book back at the station.

'Later it is, then.'

As Joe followed Harris down the stairs he thrust his hands into his pockets so that the policeman wouldn't see how much they were trembling. Just a few more seconds and he would have had the number. But now the book was out of his reach. The one simple thing his father had asked of him, and he had failed.

As Joe walked into the living room, Giles raised his eyebrows in an unspoken question. Joe shook his head and Giles replied with a look which said, *I kept him as long as I could.*

'Alright,' said Harris when they were all back where they started. 'We've got about another twenty minutes to do here, and in the meantime, no more trips upstairs. Just stay put. Then I'll phone Susie and make sure someone from CPT comes over and sorts you out. OK?'

'OK,' said Joe.

'Did you get it?' Giles asked when Harris had gone.

'Nope. Caught in the act.'

'How about we try Directory Enquiries?'

'He lives in Texas, Giles. We don't even have an address.'

'Doesn't matter. You said he was a professor, right?'

'Yes, but–'

'So, let's see here. A professor who lives in Texas. I wonder where he works?' Giles put a finger on his chin and pretended to think. 'Hmmm, that *is* tricky. Oooh, wait a minute. What about the *University* of Texas?'

Joe felt his frustration turning to hope.

'You think it'll be that easy?'

'Why not? We can check it on the internet.'

'OK, worth a try. But not here. We can't do anything here.'

'Joseph,' said Giles, putting on his most disapproving look. 'I hope you're not suggesting we disobey that nice Sergeant Harris.'

14

Lesley had thought about phoning her mother several times during the day, but each time she had stopped herself, remembering what the doctor had said.

'Just let her sleep for a while. Sleep is nature's way of allowing the body to heal.'

As she walked up the garden path, she saw that the bedroom curtains were still closed. That was a good sign. It probably meant that the tablets were working.

Pausing at the bottom of the stairs, she listened for a cough or a creak of the floorboards, something that would tell her that her mother was awake. But there was nothing, so she crept up the stairs to find that the bedroom door was firmly closed.

She was about to open it when she noticed a silver bobbin from the sewing machine on the carpet. Frowning, she picked it up and placed it on the windowsill. Then she walked across the hall to the bathroom and opened the door. The sewing machine was on top of the toilet lid again, in exactly the same place that her mother had put it before.

'Oh, *Mum*,' she whispered, massaging her eyes with the tips of her fingers. 'Whatever are we going to do with you?'

She removed the sewing machine and opened lid.

Then she heard the noise.

Thump.

She stopped, put her head on one side and listened. There it was again.

Thump. Thump. Thump.

It sounded as though it was coming from the bedroom.

Puzzled, Lesley walked across the landing and rested her fingers on the door handle.

'Mum? Are you alright?'

As suddenly as it had started, the thumping stopped.

Lesley paused.

Then she turned the handle and opened the door.

She just had time to register her mother lying face down on the carpet before something slammed into the side of her face, knocking her off her feet and sending her sprawling against the bedroom wall. As she touched the side of her head and felt the warm stickiness of her own blood, she turned and saw that something was moving towards her out of the shadows. Covering her face with her arms, she began to whimper softly, like a frightened animal.

'Help me,' she pleaded. 'Someone help me, *please*!'

The sun was still hot as Joe and Giles headed back along the canal bank, but it was a little lower in the sky now, the light falling through leaves and branches, shadows lengthening over dry earth. They passed an angler on the towpath, his transistor radio tuned to the afternoon's sports commentary.

'You alright?' asked Giles.

'Yeah, I guess so.' Joe kicked a stone and watched it skip away into a patch of nettles. 'It's just that somehow it feels like this whole thing with my dad is only the beginning. That things are going to get worse.'

Giles gestured towards an old wooden bench flanked by nettles and they both sat down.

'I felt the same way once. My father died when I was seven years old. And when it happened, I thought life could never be as good again.'

'I'm sorry, Giles,' said Joe awkwardly. 'I didn't

know.'

Giles shrugged.

'It was a long time ago now. I was away at boarding school and the head called me into his study, told me that my mother wanted to speak to me. At first I thought he meant she was there, but then he pointed to the phone on his desk.'

Giles picked up a stone and threw it into the canal. Joe watched the ripples spread out across the water, each one keeping its perfect distance from the others.

'I remember waiting for a few moments, thinking the head might leave or something, but he didn't. So I spoke to my mother and she told me my father had died. A heart attack, apparently.'

'Didn't she come and get you?' asked Joe.

'No. I guess she thought I was better off where I was. The headmaster looked at me and said, "Stiff upper lip, lad. Stiff upper lip." That was all he said. When it was over, I walked out of his office and just kept walking.'

'Where did you go?'

'Out of the door, across the playing fields and into the woods and hills. I walked for hours until it was dark. Then I found an old barn and went to sleep on the hay bales, looking up at the stars through a hole in the roof.'

Giles scratched at the bench with his fingernail and Joe knew that in his mind he was back there, reliving the moment all over again.

'I woke just as the sun was coming up. It was still dawn and I was shivering. I kept thinking about a time when I was little, before I was sent away to school, when we used to go and stay in a cottage by the sea. On warm evenings, after supper, the three of us would walk barefoot across the sand. Every now and then they would lift me up so that my feet skimmed the water. It felt like I was flying. And I just thought, I'm never going to have that again.'

Joe thought of the photograph of his mother on the fridge and realised, perhaps for the first time, that he was not the only one to have lost someone. After a while he asked, 'So what happened?'

'I walked back to school feeling cold and miserable. I knew things were never going to be the same. But as the sun came up, I realised that it's just what happens as the days go past. You walk off down the road and then, one day, you look back and everything's gone. So the trick is to just keep moving forward.'

'But don't you ever get scared?'

'Of what?'

'Of what the world's going to do to you? That one day it's going to turn round and kick you in the teeth again?'

'Sometimes, yeah. But then you can't plan for it. It's like you and your dad. When it happens, you can either let it knock you down or you can stand up and do something about it.'

'But that's the trouble,' said Joe. 'I don't know if I can, Giles. I'm not like you. I'm scared.'

'So what? Being scared doesn't matter. It's what you do when you're scared – that's what matters.'

'Just step up and smack the ball back into the stands, eh?'

'Exactly. You know, maybe the difficult stuff makes us stronger for what's to come. Maybe it helps us get to where we're meant to be.'

Joe looked at him, trying to understand.

'And where's that, Giles?'

'I'm still trying to work that one out.'

As Joe listened, he realised he had never heard Giles talk this way before. He had assumed that Giles had always been strong and confident, that things had never been difficult for him. Now, as he stared at the dark waters of the canal, he thought how we can never really know the things that lie hidden beneath the surface.

16

Milton Roberts liked it when no one else was here. He liked the sharp, clean lines of the stainless-steel surfaces, the quiet hum of the refrigeration units and the fresh, artificial smell of disinfectant.

There was no dirt, no germs.

No one to say, *Milton do this, Milton do that.*

Only the white glare of neon lights and the silence of the dead.

They never stayed long, of course. When Doctor Page had finished with them, they were taken away to be buried or burned. But even so, Milton liked to make sure that, while they were here, their stay was a comfortable one.

Every hour he checked the temperatures of the individual coolers and wrote them on his chart.

Doctor Page had told him that this was not necessary, that once a day would suffice. Milton always nodded when Doctor Page told him this, because he liked Doctor Page. Doctor Page's work was very clean and precise, and Milton appreciated that very much. But when his job was done, Doctor Page went out into the noisy, dirty world again. He didn't know that, when he was gone, Milton spent hours washing away the dirt he had brought in with him on his shoes, scrubbing and cleaning until the bright, white world was perfect again.

But now it was time to prepare the body. Doctor Page would be here soon and Milton wanted to make sure that everything was just so.

He slid open drawer number seven and was greeted by the pale, bloodless face of a man in his late forties. Milton was also in his late forties and for a moment this fact made him uncomfortable. He imagined himself lying still, all thoughts and desires blown away like seeds from a dandelion clock, leaving only this object, this strange, detached thing with no more life than the cold steel table or the floor upon which he stood.

But Milton did not allow himself to dwell upon these matters, for there was work to be done.

He pulled the drawer out to its full extent, unzipped the body bag and checked the tag on the corpse's big toe.

William Sims.

Milton looked at his job sheet to make sure that

the name corresponded with the one he had written down. Satisfied that it did, he transferred the body to the trolley and wheeled it across to the post-mortem table. Milton knew that most people would find this distasteful, this manhandling of a dead person. Most people would rather not know about such things, because it would remind them of their own mortality. But although Milton had been frightened the first time, he now found himself strangely comforted by the fact that dead people were so cold, so stiff, so unfeeling. It made him think that life was a magical thing, something which attached itself to plants in springtime and babies when they were born. And when winter came, when the ties that bound it were broken, it disappeared, leaving only the blackened, frosted stems in empty flowerbeds and these strange pieces of meat, distant and separate from the things they once were.

Milton washed the body, weighed and measured it, wrote *83 kg / 182 cm* on the record sheet. He removed the plastic bags from the hands, took swabs from the fingernails, then placed the body block beneath the back to raise the chest, ready for Doctor Page's examination. It was at this point that he noticed the angry red wound across the patient's neck, and the purple bruising around it.

Milton nodded to himself, as if answering a question asked by an imaginary onlooker. 'What we have here,' he said into the cool silence of the morgue, 'is a definite case of homicide.'

Milton smiled, imagining that he was the one carrying out the post-mortem.

Milton Roberts, the world famous pathologist.

'Homicide, eh?' asked an amused voice behind him. 'Well let's see if I agree with you, shall we?'

Milton turned to see Doctor Page standing behind him and blushed a deep crimson.

'I'm sorry Doctor Page, I was just—'

'Please,' said Doctor Page, holding up his hands. 'No need to apologise. I'm just pleased that you are interested enough to make a diagnosis.' He paused, considering something.

'Tell me. How long have you been working as an assistant here?'

'Eighteen years,' said Milton.

'Eighteen years. And the last three with me?'

'Yes, sir.' Milton looked at the floor as he added, 'They have been three very instructive years too, Doctor Page. I have learned a great deal from watching your work.'

Doctor Page smiled.

'Well then. Let's see how much you have learned, shall we?'

Milton's heart fluttered. Surely Doctor Page

could not mean what he thought he meant?

'Doctor Page?'

Doctor Page gestured towards the tray of surgical instruments shining silver beneath the lights.

'Would you like to make the first incision for me? Open up the chest cavity?'

Milton was so taken aback by this that at first he was unable to speak. Biting his lip, he held on to the table for support. Then he looked at Doctor Page – this man who was giving him a chance to do something worthwhile at last – and smiled shyly, like a child invited to perform in front of the grown-ups.

'Yes,' he said. 'I would like that very much.'

Forty-five minutes later Milton Roberts was exhausted. The work had been both exacting and difficult at times, but it was not this which had taken his energy. Rather it was his wish, his determination to repay Doctor Page's faith in him that had left him feeling as though he had not slept in days. The pressure not to fail, to carry out an impressively faultless procedure, had been immense. But under the watchful eye of Doctor Page he had successfully opened the body cavity and assisted him in the removal of the internal organs, helping him to weigh and replace them. Doctor Page had even allowed him to use the bone cutter to open the ribcage. It was a procedure he had witnessed many times, but never imagined that one day he would carry out himself.

It really had been the most remarkable day.

'Well done, Milton,' said Doctor Page. 'You've done a good job here.'

Milton smiled.

'Thank you, Doctor Page,' he said. 'Thank you very much.'

'Alright,' said Doctor Page. 'Replace the chest flap if you will. It's about time we had a look at what caused this poor man's problems in the first place. Time to discover if your initial theory was right.'

Milton took a deep breath and pulled the chest flap – which had been draped over the face – back into place.

'Now that is interesting,' said Doctor Page, framing the man's face with gloved hands and using his thumbs to tip the head back a fraction. 'Very interesting indeed.'

Milton leaned forward to get a better look and saw that the wound in the man's neck was even longer than he had first supposed.

'What do you make of that then, eh?'

'I would guess that the trauma to the neck was definitely the cause of death,' offered Milton in a hushed voice.

'Well,' said Doctor Page, 'I don't think you'd find many people who would disagree with you on that one. But look here. Look at this. What do you notice?'

Milton looked more closely and saw the rough, ragged edges of the wound.

'Well, it's not a clean cut.'

'You're right,' said Doctor Page, much to Milton's relief. 'Not a clean cut at all. In fact,' he added, following the line of the cut with his finger, 'what we have here is the kind of thing you might expect to find after an attack by a wild animal of some description. Look. See? Here.'

He traced the outline of the wound with his finger, drawing Milton's attention to the line of serrated flesh.

'If I didn't know better, I'd say that these were bite marks.'

'Bite marks?' Milton echoed in surprise.

'I know,' said Page, taking a swab and running it along the edge of the wound. 'It sounds unlikely, doesn't it? But look at the pattern of them. It looks as if something – or someone – just went crazy and tore his throat out.'

'With what?' asked Milton, feeling pleased that Doctor Page valued him enough to discuss such details with him.

'Do you know,' replied Doctor Page, shaking his head, 'for the first time in my life, I have absolutely no idea.'

17

Detective Sergeant Harris was already having a bad day, and now it was showing every sign of getting worse. McDonald was refusing to answer questions without a solicitor being present, and now the post-mortem report was making his life even harder. He'd asked for it to be sent as soon as it was written, and he was already beginning to wish that he hadn't.

Apparently the cause of death was *'Cardiac arrest as a result of unspecified trauma to the carotid artery and massive blood loss.'*

In other words, someone had cut Sims's throat and he'd lost so much blood that the poor guy had suffered a heart attack.

But the phrase 'unspecified trauma' meant the forensic guys couldn't figure out exactly how his throat had been cut. So any chance of matching a weapon to the wound was slim, to say the least. Then there was the part about 'massive blood loss'.

He'd been on enough murder investigations to know that cutting someone's throat was a pretty messy business. But a thorough search of McDonald's house and car hadn't managed to turn up a single speck of blood.

Harris sighed.

It didn't make any sense.

If McDonald had killed Sims, there would have been blood on his clothing. And lots of it.

Which left only two possible conclusions.

One: McDonald had managed to get rid of his clothing and remove all traces of blood from himself and his car.

Two: he was innocent.

But how could he be?

Harris considered the facts.

CCTV security cameras covered all the entrances to the building. They showed him entering at 10.14 p.m. and leaving at 10.47 p.m.

No one else entered or left the building until 6.59 a.m. the following morning, when the cleaning staff arrived and a hysterical emergency call was logged at 7.09.

The post-mortem put the time of death in a three-hour 'bracket of probability', between 10 p.m. and 1.00 a.m.

Given that McDonald stated Sims was still alive

when he left at 10.47 p.m., he was either lying or Sims died some time between 10.47 p.m. and 1.00 a.m., when there was no one else in the building.

There was also the matter of a recent interview with a colleague who worked in the next room. He had heard shouting during the afternoon and observed, in his words, Sims and McDonald 'having some kind of argument' but he had decided to leave them to it.

Harris took a sip of coffee and looked around at his colleagues, all of them hunched over their computer keyboards, tapping away at their reports.

The job had changed so much since the old days, when you could just pull bad guys off the street and have them banged up behind bars before they even knew what had hit them.

Nowadays it was all about targets and paperwork.

Harris stared at the old rubber plant in the corner and remembered how fresh and green it had looked when it first arrived. Now its leaves sagged and it was covered in dust; a pale resemblance of the thing it used to be.

The phone rang and, with a sigh, Harris picked it up.

'Yes, sir,' he said without enthusiasm. 'I'll be right there.'

* * *

'Shut the door,' said Superintendent Reeve as Harris stepped into the office. His tone didn't make Harris feel too hopeful about what was coming next.

Reeve picked up a folder and threw it across the table.

'You've read this, I take it?'

Harris saw that it was the post-mortem report and nodded.

'And you're still hoping to make a case against McDonald?'

Harris shrugged.

'It's still only a provisional report.'

'Yes I know, Sergeant. And it's provisionally saying that we don't know a damn thing.'

'At this stage, maybe. But it's early days.'

'Sergeant Harris, I don't want to hear any more about early days or provisional reports. The deceased's wife has already spoken to the press and this is going to be all over the papers tomorrow. So I want it sorted, and I want it sorted now. Is that clear?'

'Crystal,' said Harris.

The phone on his desk rang and Reeve clamped it to his ear, glaring at Harris as he paced up and down.

'Alright. Keep a lid on it until we find out exactly what's going on. But listen: the moment you know anything, let me know. In the meantime I'll send someone over.'

Reeve replaced the receiver and looked at Harris.

'There's just been a call to a house in Rose Gardens. Attempted murder. Two women, both in a bad way, one with serious throat injuries. Tell me something, Sergeant Harris. Where is your Mr McDonald at the moment?'

Harris shrugged. 'As far as I know, he's down in the cells.'

'Right. Well your first job is to make sure he's still there. Your second is to get over to this place in Rose Gardens and see if there are any similarities. And if there are, Sergeant Harris, then I think we can be sure of at least one thing.'

'What's that?' asked Harris.

Superintendent Reeve sat down and closed the folder.

'You're going to have to find yourself a new tree to bark up,' he said.

18

The moment Harris turned the corner into Rose Gardens he knew that life was about to get a whole lot more complicated. Two police cars, an ambulance and a line of blue and white tape surrounding the house meant they weren't going to be able to keep things under wraps much longer. The reporters would come sniffing about like dogs around a rubbish bin, asking, *Is there some kind of connection here? Is there a madman in our midst?*

Then Superintendent Reeve would come looking for him, demanding answers. And right now, Harris didn't have any to give him.

'Alright, Tony?' he asked as the uniformed officer stepped back to let him through. 'Anything I should know?'

The officer pointed towards the ambulance. 'They're just taking one of them away now.'

Harris watched the ambulance pull away from

the kerb, its blue lights flashing.

'One of them?'

'The old lady who lives here. A Mrs Lewis.'

'Is she still alive?'

'Just about. But I wouldn't like to say for how long. She looked in a bad way.'

'So what happened?'

'No idea, I'm afraid. They're just in the process of getting a statement.'

'From whom?'

'From the daughter, I think.'

'The daughter?'

'A Mrs Lesley Croft.'

Harris stood in the hallway listening to the voices upstairs. There was no sign of a forced entry, so he went to check on the kitchen. Two cups were set out neatly next to the kettle and the windows were closed and intact. Beyond the kitchen was a small utility room with a washing machine, a drier and a couple of shelves holding up some dusty geraniums. The key was in the back door, and the back door was locked.

OK, thought Harris, his mind already half made up. *Time to meet the daughter.*

Lesley Croft was sitting on the edge of the bed when he got there. Her blouse was ripped and, although the paramedics had bandaged up her arms, he could see the bloodstains on her jeans. If the injuries were self-inflicted, then she had done a pretty good job.

'Detective Sergeant Harris,' he said by way of introduction.

The woman looked up. 'Hello,' she said. 'Have you caught them yet?'

Harris frowned.

'Caught who?'

'You know. *Them*.'

Harris was about to ask what she meant when Wallace, another of the uniformed guys, touched him on the arm.

'Sir? Can I have a word?'

Harris followed him out into the hallway and raised his eyebrows impatiently.

'The thing is, sir,' Wallace said in a low voice, 'I don't know if she's all there.'

'Meaning?'

'Meaning,' said Wallace, tapping the side of his head, 'that I think she may be a bit, you know, doolally.'

'Oh yeah?' said Harris, hoping this might explain things. If Lesley Croft really was crazy then it would be a pretty straightforward case and he could get back to nailing McDonald. 'What makes you say that?'

'She keeps going on about this thing that came into the house and attacked her. Said it was in the bedroom when she arrived.'

OK, thought Harris. *That simplifies things.* The woman was clearly mad and now she was going to make everyone's lives easier by proving it.

'You reckon she did it, then?'

Wallace shrugged. 'Too early to say. But there's no sign of a break-in, nothing missing, and we've got an old lady with her throat cut and a daughter talking about something trying to kill her. I mean, it's classic crazy stuff, isn't it?'

'Sounds that way. Who phoned the emergency services?'

'The daughter, I think.'

'Alright, we'll need a transcript of that.'

Harris looked back towards the bedroom and wondered, not for the first time, what made people do such terrible things. If he'd seen her out on the street he'd have thought: ordinary, middle-aged woman with an ordinary, middle-aged life. But somewhere along the line, something inside her had flipped. Now she was probably looking at spending the rest of her life in a secure institution.

It was sad, no doubt about it. But Harris had seen enough sadness in this job to know that you couldn't let it touch you.

'Any sign of a weapon?'

'Slight problem there,' said Wallace awkwardly. 'We haven't managed to find one yet.'

'Perhaps,' suggested Harris, 'you haven't looked hard enough.'

Wallace shrugged. 'Perhaps. But we've looked in all the obvious places, and there's nothing so far.'

'Alright,' said Harris. 'As soon as you find anything, let me know.'

He turned and walked back into the bedroom.

'Lesley?' he said. 'May I speak with you for a moment?'

Signalling for the other police officer to leave, he crouched down so that Lesley's face was level with his own. She sat on the edge of the bed, staring at the carpet and twisting her hands in her lap.

'They don't believe me,' she said. 'No one does.'

'About what?

'About what happened. They think I did it.'

'And did you?'

For the first time, Lesley lifted her head and looked Harris in the eye.

'No,' she said. 'Of course not.'

Harris wasn't sure why, but there was something in the way she said it that made him inclined to believe her.

'Then perhaps,' he said gently, 'you'd like to tell

me what did happen.'

'What's the point?' Lesley folded her arms across her chest as if this simple act might keep Harris and the rest of the world at bay. 'You won't believe me either.'

'Well,' said Harris, 'we're never going to know that unless you give it a try.'

Lesley slid her hands into her lap once more and stared at a patch of sunlight on the wall.

'What's your name?' she asked after a while.

'Harris,' said Harris. 'Detective Sergeant Harris.'

'No. I mean your *real* name.'

Harris stood up and walked to the window. Down in the street, a small terrier was peeing contentedly against the wheel of a police car.

'Raymond,' he said. 'Ray for short.'

'Ray,' she said. 'That's a nice name.'

Harris said nothing, waiting for her to continue.

'Tell me something, Ray. What would you do if you saw a monster?'

'You mean like King Kong? Something like that?'

'No. I mean something from the darkest, most frightening parts of your mind. Something you thought only existed in nightmares.'

Harris looked at her. 'I guess I'd think, maybe I should see a doctor.'

'You wouldn't believe it then?'

'No.'

'Why not?'

'Because monsters don't exist, Lesley. They're a product of our imaginations.'

'You see? That's why you're not going to believe me.'

'Why?'

'Because, Ray, monsters do exist. I've seen one and it was horrible. I don't expect you to believe me because I can hardly believe it myself. But that's what it was, I swear. It almost killed my mother. And then it tried to kill me. All I can say is, thank God for electricity.' She nodded towards the bedside lamp that lay smashed in pieces on the floor. 'Hitting it with that thing saved my life.'

Harris folded his arms and leaned back against the wall. He looked around at all the things that were real – the glass perfume bottles on the dresser, the pots of make-up and moisturiser, the broken lamp, the bedside table – and these things told him that the world was too ordinary, too familiar to allow the existence of Lesley Croft's monsters. But as he watched her weeping softly, sitting alone on the bed with her arms bandaged up, he began to feel sorry for her. She wasn't like the others, the mean, selfish people who committed their crimes because of greed or jealousy, anger or hatred.

She seemed lost and afraid, as if she really believed that her nightmares were coming true.

She needed help.

Stepping over the broken lamp, Harris sat next to her and put his hand on her arm.

'We should get you to a hospital,' he said. 'Get you fixed up.'

Lesley wiped her eyes and nodded, resigning herself to the situation. And as Harris patted her on the shoulder and got up to go, she said, 'You seem like a decent man, Ray. So take my advice and stay away from bathrooms for a while, OK?'

The words stopped Harris in his tracks.

'What did you say?' he asked.

'The bathroom,' she said. 'That's where it came from. I tried to tell the others, but they didn't listen. They didn't want to know.'

Harris walked across the landing, pushed open the door into the bathroom and looked at the damp trail across the bathroom carpet.

'That's another weird thing,' said Wallace, following him in. 'I mean, why would anyone wash their hands in the toilet?'

But as Harris peered down into the crimson water of the toilet bowl, he remembered the photographs taken at the university and suddenly felt very afraid.

'Get everyone out of here,' he said, gripping the edge of the sink. 'Get them out of here now.'

And as Wallace turned to protest, he bundled him out of the room, slammed the door shut and flipped open his phone.

'Get me Superintendent Reeve,' he said. 'And tell him that it's urgent.'

'There has to be some kind of picture,' said Giles, 'a puzzle where all the reasons for what's happened just fit together. At the moment we don't know what it looks like. But the more pieces of the puzzle we find, the easier it will be.'

'But that's what the police are doing, isn't it?' asked Joe. 'Putting the puzzle together?'

'Maybe. But I reckon they're picking all the wrong pieces. And if they can't pick the right ones, then it's up to us to do it for them.'

But Joe had stopped listening.

He was staring at the far side of the canal.

'Look,' he whispered. 'Over there.'

Giles followed his gaze to an uneven patch of water beneath the willows. As they watched, there was a splash and then a dark shape began moving towards them at speed beneath the surface. As it approached the bank it suddenly changed direction

and blurred into shadow before disappearing altogether.

'What was *that*?' asked Giles.

'Looked like an eel,' said Joe.

'No way. Did you see how fast it moved?'

'Well what, then?'

'I don't know.'

'I'm going to go and get my camera,' said Giles
excitedly, 'see if I can get a picture. Do you want to
stay here? I'll only be a few minutes.'

'OK,' said Joe. 'No problem.'

As Giles ran off down the towpath Joe watched
the sunlight sparkle across the water and felt as
though the world was mocking him. *Everything you
believed in was an illusion*, it seemed to be saying. *The
world is not the way you thought it was. Not the way you
thought it was at all . . .*

Giles had only been gone a couple of minutes when
Joe heard the sound; a rustling noise behind him, as
though something was moving at speed through the
bushes.

Somewhere in the distance, a dog barked.

Joe thought about the strange shape he had seen
in the canal and began to feel uneasy. For a moment
he considered trying to catch up with Giles but
then, as he listened, the sound stopped again. All he

could hear was the warble of birdsong floating through the warm air and the distant hum of a lawnmower. Although he was still a little afraid, he remembered what Giles had said about being at school on that summer morning, walking without fear towards an uncertain future.

This is a test, he thought, *a chance to be more like Giles. To face up to whatever life throws at me.*

Clenching his fists, he took a step towards the tangle of brambles that grew along the towpath. He stopped and listened. Then he took another step forward, and another.

Suddenly there was a scrabble of movement and a rabbit broke cover, flying out of the bushes in a flurry of dust. Joe's heart pounded as the rabbit ran away down the path, but then he began to smile at the ridiculousness of his fears. Perhaps, he thought, the world was not such a threatening place after all. There were usually simple explanations for the things that frightened you. You just had to know where to look.

Maybe tomorrow they'd get in touch with Dave Moreton and find that the whole thing had been a terrible mistake.

And then, maybe, his dad would come home.

He turned back towards the bench, deciding he would just sit there quietly until Giles returned.

But then he stopped.

For there, in the centre of the path, was a huge snake-like creature, writhing and coiling around itself so that small pieces of earth stuck to the wet, slippery surface of its skin. It was dark green, like a serpent from an ancient fairy-tale, thicker than a drainpipe and over a metre of solid, squirming muscle. As Joe nervously took a step backwards it stopped moving and turned to face him. The front of its head was tapered, more like a worm than a snake, but as it uncoiled and raised itself from the ground, two dark red slits appeared in the side of its head, widening into eyes. Beneath them the beast's slimy flesh split open to reveal a circle of razor sharp teeth.

As Joe backed nervously away the serpent slithered forward so that the distance between them never altered.

'My God,' Joe whispered. 'What is *that*?'

Snatching up a stone, he flung it at the creature, striking it low on the body. It flinched briefly and moved back. Then it rose up onto the tip of its tail and launched itself at him.

Joe turned and ran. He could hear it slithering through the dust behind him, gaining on him with every second. He turned towards the willow that grew by the water's edge and, with a sob of fear, plunged through the green curtain of branches, scrabbling at the trunk as he tried to pull himself clear of the ground. But with an angry hiss, the creature reared up and slammed its head into his calf muscle. He fell back with a shriek of pain, hitting the ground with a thump that knocked all the wind out of him. He turned to see the hideous serpent thrashing its tail across the ground as it sank its teeth deeper into his leg, but somehow he managed to twist round and bring his heel down hard onto its head. The pressure on his leg slackened as he hammered his heel down again and again until finally the beast released its grip and retreated a couple of feet.

'Get away from me,' he hissed, his lips drawing back in disgust. But as the serpent slithered through the dust towards him again, he knew it wasn't finished with him.

This time it was moving in for the kill.

Staggering to his feet, he searched around for a weapon, but before he could move the creature flung itself forward, looping its tail around his leg and wriggling up towards his throat. He dug his nails into the cold, wet flesh but the skin was so slippery that it slid from his grasp and the serpent lashed out again, its sharp teeth nuzzling at his neck.

Stumbling back under its weight, Joe tried to

reach for a fallen branch with his free foot, but it was too far away and his shoe scraped uselessly across the dry ground. In a final act of desperation he twisted round, grabbed the tree trunk and threw himself at it, slamming the creature against the rough bark. As it tried to wriggle free he hurled himself at it again and this time it squelched like a wet flannel before falling to the floor. As it twisted round to face him once more, he jumped sideways and snatched up the branch.

For a moment the serpent seemed to hesitate. Its eyes narrowed into slits and it moved lower, coiling like a steel spring. Then without warning it leapt forward and knocked him to the ground. As the branch flew from his grasp, Joe curled himself up into a ball and put his hands over his face, desperate to protect himself from further attack. But then he heard the sound of someone running; there was a shout, a loud crack and Joe peered through his fingers to see Giles standing over him, brandishing a cricket bat.

'Hang on,' said Giles, holding up a finger. 'I think it's coming back.'

Joe jumped to his feet and saw the monstrous animal heading towards them once again.

'Give me that,' he said. Then, grabbing the bat from Giles, he stepped forward and swung it so hard that the serpent twisted up into the air like a piece of living rope. He watched it land on the grass, bounce once and then slither back towards the canal.

'Blimey,' said Giles, turning to Joe with a look of astonishment on his face. 'What the hell was that?'

'It attacked me just after you left,' said Joe. He winced and put a hand on Giles's shoulder to steady himself. 'I think it came from the canal.'

'Are you OK?' asked Giles, seeing the pain in his eyes.

'Yeah, I think so.' Joe dropped the cricket bat and pulled up his trouser leg, revealing a bloody circle of puncture wounds. 'Damn thing went for my leg.'

'Come on,' said Giles, putting an arm round his shoulder. 'Let's get back to the house and get you cleaned up.'

'Maybe we should call the police,' suggested Joe, looking anxiously towards the canal. 'It might come back.'

'Well, it might,' said Giles, picking up his cricket bat, 'but then do you really want Harris and his gang tramping all over the place, asking lots of questions?'

'Maybe not,' said Joe. 'Perhaps we should try and track down this Moreton guy first.'

As they walked back towards the house, Giles said, 'You know, you should really take up cricket.

That was one helluva hit.'

In spite of the pain, Joe smiled.

'Smacked it all the way into the stands,' he said.

20

As they entered the kitchen Joe saw that the work-tops were all top of the range – sparkly black granite and polished steel. It was the biggest kitchen he had ever seen. Beyond it was a huge living room with deep carpets, polished wood and huge windows which allowed the light to flood in. Two antique swords were fixed to the wall above a big stone fireplace, their silver blades crossing in a neat 'X'.

As Joe sat down on a chair next to the Aga, Giles's mother appeared in the doorway. She was dressed in a powder blue tracksuit, blinking in the sunlight as though she had just got out of bed.

'Giles, darling – what on earth has happened?'

'There's been a bit of an accident,' said Giles. 'Nothing to worry about. But we're going to need the first-aid kit.'

Mrs Barclay's hands fluttered up to her face as she

saw Joe's bloodied leg. Then she turned away and picked up a half-empty wine glass from the kitchen table. 'Would anyone like a drink?' she asked. 'I've got a really nice Chablis on the go.'

'Mum,' said Giles, taking the wine glass from her fingers and placing it back on the table. 'It's four in the afternoon.'

'Well, you know what they say,' she replied, picking up the wine glass again. 'Over the bottle, many a friend is found.'

'Mum please,' said Giles calmly, fetching a green plastic first-aid box from one of the cupboards. 'I'm trying to sort Joe's leg out here.'

'Right,' said Mrs Barclay, 'well in that case I shall leave you to it.'

And with that she turned on her heel and walked out of the room.

'Take no notice,' said Giles, popping open the catches on the first-aid kit. 'She's had a bit of a time of it recently, what with my stepfather leaving and everything. Good riddance, I say.'

'Why?' asked Joe. 'Didn't you like him?'

'No I didn't. He pretended he loved her, but all he really wanted was a well-behaved, plastic dolly. Someone to look good on his arm at business functions. He made her go on a diet, have her hair and nails done twice a month and stopped her doing the one thing that she really loved.'

'Which was what?'

'Rebuilding old cars.' Giles took out a bottle of antiseptic and placed it on the kitchen counter. 'One of my earliest memories is seeing her slide out from beneath some old banger, all covered in oil. My grandad used to say she was better than any of his mechanics.'

'Really?' Joe tried to picture the designer-clad Mrs Barclay getting oil on her perfectly manicured nails. 'I can't imagine that.'

'No, nor could my stepfather. He said it wasn't ladylike to do that kind of thing. And because he had lots of money, they always had new cars and so she never had any reason to mend them. But sometimes I look at old photos of her, all covered in oil and holding a spanner, and she's just got the biggest smile on her face. And I realise she never smiles that way any more.'

Joe watched Giles take out an assortment of gauze, bandages and plasters and thought about all the cuts and scars which people couldn't see; the ones which took longest to heal.

'OK, Joe,' said Giles, kneeling down with a ball of cotton wool in one hand and a bottle of antiseptic in the other. 'This might sting a bit. But it'll do you good.'

Joe shut his eyes, clenching his fists each time the cotton wool touched his broken skin. But he didn't cry out or make a sound. He was facing up to the world, because that was the only way you got through it.

'So what do you think it was?' asked Giles as he bustled around the kitchen making supper. 'Do you think it's definitely the same thing we saw in the canal?'

Joe thought about the long dark shape he had seen sliding beneath the water and the strange creature that had attacked him. 'I think it's got to be,' he said. 'It was all wet and slimy, like an eel or something.'

'Strange kind of eel though, jumping out of canals and biting people.'

'I know. And did you see the size of it?'

'Maybe it escaped from a zoo or somewhere.'

Joe shook his head. 'I've been to a few zoos in my time, but I've never seen anything like that. Maybe we should try and get hold of this Dave Moreton and then tell someone. I don't think we can just leave it. That thing was vicious.'

'Alright,' said Giles, setting some knives and forks on the table. 'But let's have something to eat first. I'm starving.'

* * *

'Just a little snack to get your strength up,' Giles said as Joe sat at the table. 'Mozzarella cheese and tomato on a bed of rocket with an olive oil and balsamic vinegar dressing. And some brown bread and butter to go with it.'

'Wow,' said Joe. 'I was expecting baked beans or something.'

'Baked beans?' said Giles. 'What on earth are those?'

Joe was about to reply when he realised that Giles was joking. So instead he said, 'I've no idea. Something normal people eat, I think.'

Giles chuckled and sat down at the far end of the oak table, at which point his mother appeared in the doorway.

'Having a dinner party, darling?' she asked, leaning on the door frame.

Giles immediately pushed his chair back and went over to her.

'Come and sit down,' he said. 'I've made some for you too.'

He tried to guide her to the end of the dinner table, but she shrugged him off and sat opposite Joe.

'Hello,' she said, smiling and resting her chin on the palm of her hand. 'Having fun?'

Joe looked into Mrs Barclay's eyes and saw that

she seemed lost, like a small child.

'Yes thank you, Mrs Barclay,' he said. 'It's very kind of you to have me here.'

'Please,' said Mrs Barclay, keeping her eyes fixed on him as she lifted a slice of cheese on the end of her fork. 'Call me Linda. I would introduce you to Giles's stepfather, but he ran off to America with his secretary.'

'Mum,' said Giles.

For a few moments no one spoke and there was just the squeak and scrape of cutlery on china. Joe saw Giles's mum watching him as he lifted the fork to his mouth.

'Your hands are trembling,' she said. 'Are you alright?'

Joe looked at Giles and saw that he was shaking his head.

'I just slipped,' he said, 'that's all.'

'Well you look scared to me. Are you sure you're OK?'

Joe nodded. 'Really. I'm fine.'

Mrs Barclay finished her wine and stared into the empty glass. 'When I was little,' she said, 'I was scared of the dark, so my father used to come and sit on the end of my bed. He told me that evenings were his favourite part of the day.'

She poured herself another glass of wine, then

got up and walked across to the French windows.

'He said he liked the way that all the dirt and grime got hidden away, covered in a thick blanket so that all you could see were the stars. He said that darkness was a beautiful thing, because it helped you see the light more clearly. Perhaps that's what we all need.' She paused and took another sip of wine. 'Just someone to sit on the end of our bed when the night comes.'

She stared through the open windows and watched the patterns of weak sunlight dapple the lawn. 'Because sometimes you look up and there are no stars at all.'

Giles got up and put his arm round her shoulders.

'Maybe you can't see them,' he said, 'but the stars are still there.'

21

After they'd eaten, Joe followed Giles across the entrance hall and up the twisting oak staircase. The evening sun shone through the landing window, dappling the plum-coloured carpet and sparkling through the glass chandelier that hung above the hallway.

As Giles opened the door to his bedroom, Joe heard a strange buzzing sound which seemed to be coming from the fireplace.

'What's that noise?' he asked.

'You don't want to know,' said Giles, smiling and switching on his computer.

'Yeah I do. What is it?'

'Wasps.'

'Wasps?' Joe looked nervously at the fireplace. 'You're kidding. Up there?'

'Yup. They've made a nest at the top of the chimney. You don't like 'em much, do you?'

'I hate them. Don't you?'

Giles shrugged.

'I'm not bothered. As long as they're up there and I'm down here, we get along just fine.'

Joe watched Giles type 'University of Texas' into the search engine and wondered how he could sleep at night when there was a chance that a nestful of wasps might come crashing down into his bedroom.

But then, that was exactly the point, wasn't it?

Giles wouldn't allow himself to worry about it.

'There,' said Joe, pointing to the screen as the *University of Texas at Austin* home page came up. 'Staff.'

Giles clicked on the *About Us* link, but although there were lists of sections where you could find out about Administration, Training, Policies and Regulations, there was nothing listing actual names.

'Go back to the home page,' Joe suggested.

Giles brought the home page up again and Joe checked the headings along the top.

'Try *Directory*.'

Giles clicked on *Directory* and a new screen came up with the heading *Student, Staff and Faculty Directory*. Beneath it was a white rectangular search box.

'Good thinking,' said Giles. 'What's his name

again?'

'Dave Moreton.'

Giles typed in Moreton's name. 'OK, Davey boy,' he muttered. 'Be there, be there, be there . . .'

A new screen appeared. In blue, across the top, were the words: Search returned 1 close match. Below it, written in red, was one line:

David S. Moreton. Faculty: School of Integrated Biology, College of Natural Sciences.

'Yes!' said Joe, clenching his fist. 'That's him. That's our man.'

Giles clicked on the name and a page came up giving his office address, home address and contact details for both.

He took out his mobile and handed it to Joe. 'There you go,' he said. 'Time you two had a little conversation, I think.'

Joe stared at the phone for a moment, amazed that they had got to this point so quickly. Giles nodded encouragingly.

'Go on. Go for it.'

Joe keyed in the digits on the screen and heard a woman's voice telling him the number had not been recognised. He looked at Giles. 'I can't get through,' he said.

Giles checked the number again.

'You need the international code first. Two zeros and a one.'

Joe punched the numbers in and this time he heard the ring tone. There was a click at the other end and then a recorded American voice:

'I'm sorry, I'm not at my desk right now. But if you leave your name and number, I'll call back as soon as I can.'

There was a beep, followed by the hiss of an answer machine.

Joe pressed disconnect and the phone went dead.

'Problem?'

'He's not there.'

'Try his home number.'

'You think?'

Giles shrugged. 'Worth a shot.'

Joe pressed the new numbers into his phone and waited.

'Hello?' said a woman's voice. 'This is Sarah Moreton.'

For a moment Joe was so taken aback that he didn't reply.

'Hello? Who is this, please?'

'Oh, ummm . . . Hi. My name's Joe. Joe McDonald. You don't know me, but I really need to speak to Professor Moreton, if that's possible.'

'I'm afraid Professor Moreton isn't here right now.' The woman's voice sounded uncertain. 'Can I ask what this is in connection with?'

'It's to do with someone called William Sims,' said Joe. 'My father asked me to speak to Professor Moreton urgently.'

'I'm sorry, but I'm afraid Professor Moreton won't be home for a few days. He's away in Mexico. Perhaps you'd like to try again when he comes back?'

'I don't suppose,' said Joe, 'that there is any way I could contact him? I really need to talk to him.'

'Hmm,' said the woman. 'Well now you've got me intrigued.' She left space for Joe to supply more information, but when he remained silent it was she who spoke again.

'It's possible to contact him in Mexico,' she said, 'although as I don't know who you are, I wouldn't feel comfortable giving you his number. But I'm happy to give him yours and pass on a message. Then he can decide whether or not he wants to speak to you. OK?'

'OK,' said Joe. 'That sounds good. But could you tell him it's urgent?'

After he had given her the number he handed the phone back to Giles and stood by the bedroom window. The sun was sinking down behind the trees, colouring the sky red and throwing long shadows across the lawn. He thought of his father alone in a police cell, and wondered when he would see him again.

'So what did she say?' Giles asked.

'She said he'd call when he got round to it. So maybe he will. And maybe he won't.'

'Hang on to it,' said Giles, handing the phone back to Joe. 'He'll call, I know he will.'

But as Joe slipped the phone into his pocket, he heard a desperate, high-pitched noise coming from downstairs and realised that it was the sound of someone screaming.

'Wait!' called Joe as Giles flew out of the door. 'Wait for me!' But by the time he got to the doorway, Giles was already running down the stairs.

For a moment Joe hesitated, his recent encounter with the strange creature still fresh in his mind. But as he listened to the screams it became obvious that Giles's mother was going to need all the help she could get. Swallowing his fear, he walked out onto the landing and peered over the banisters. A side door into the garden had been left open and there was a faint trail of slime leading across the hall carpet. As Joe made his way nervously down the stairs he heard shouts and screams from the living room, followed by the crash of something heavy falling over. Picking up a golfing umbrella from beneath the coat stand, he walked towards the living room, keeping his eyes firmly fixed on the open doorway.

'Giles, get it out of here!' Giles's mother screamed. '*Please!* Make it go away!' There was another loud crash and then she began screeching like a wounded animal.

Gripping the umbrella, Joe ran the last few metres to the living room. He could see Giles's mother through the open door, lying in the corner with her tracksuit ripped and the carpet around her stained with blood. As he entered the room he saw a green blur and recognised the serpent from the canal, zigzagging its way across the carpet. It was heading straight for Giles, who lay against the French windows clutching the cricket bat in his hand. He was bleeding from a cut on the side of his face and Joe guessed he must have fallen and banged his head. One thing was clear: if he didn't do something fast, Giles and his mother were going to die.

Lifting the umbrella high in the air, Joe ran forward and brought it down with all his strength onto the creature's head. As it twisted round, jerking and twitching, he swung the umbrella hard and caught it with the pointed steel tip. The serpent emitted an unearthly, high-pitched shriek and fell back onto the carpet before wriggling round to face him again.

Joe knew it was up to him now.

If he didn't destroy this thing, they were all dead.

Gritting his teeth, he stepped forward and swung the umbrella once more, this time aiming for the serpent's head. But its reactions were too fast; it had already learned from experience and moved quickly out of harm's way. Then it began sliding across the carpet towards him again.

It was horrifying, relentless. Joe realised that it wasn't going to stop, that it would keep on attacking, searching for a weakness until eventually it found a way through. But then, as he staggered back into the middle of the room, his eyes fell upon the swords above the mantelpiece. Leaping sideways into the hearth, he ripped one from the wall. As the creature lunged forward he swung the blade around in a wide arc, chopping it clean in half with a loud, sickening squelch. As the top section flew off and slammed into the wall, the bottom half flopped backwards and began writhing and twitching across the carpet. Screwing his face up in disgust, Joe ran forward and kicked the twisting mass through the French windows. Then he dropped the sword, ran across the room and picked up the other half, hurling it out after the first. As it skidded across the patio he grabbed the handles of the French windows and slammed them shut. He watched for a moment as the two halves continued to squirm across the concrete slabs, the rear half climbing blindly up a pile of bricks like some grotesque mountaineer before reaching the summit and tumbling down the other side. He pulled the curtains to shut out the nightmare and sank to his knees beside Giles.

'Giles!' he shouted, seizing him by the shoulders. 'Giles, wake up!'

Giles sat up, blinked, then put a hand to the side of his head. 'Oh God,' he said, struggling to his feet. '*Mum!*'

Staggering across the carpet, he knelt beside his mother and pulled off his shirt, tying it around the torn, ragged flesh of her arm.

'Stay there,' said Joe. 'Stay with her and I'll call an ambulance.' As he turned to go, he saw the crimson stain blossom like a rose and hoped he wasn't too late.

22

Stumbling into the hallway, Joe punched in the emergency numbers and hurriedly gave his address. Noticing that the side door was still open, he ran over and slammed it shut. He was about to return to the living room when he felt a buzzing in his pocket. Realising that he still had Giles's phone, he pulled it out and flipped open the cover.

'Hello? Joe McDonald speaking.'

'Joe. Good to talk to you.'

There was a slight time delay, but Joe detected an American accent.

'Professor Moreton?'

'Yeah, that's me. My wife tells me you've been wanting to track me down.'

'That's right,' said Joe, his head still spinning. He closed his eyes and tried to concentrate. 'Professor, I need to ask you something.'

'Well, before you do,' said Moreton, 'can I ask

who you are? I mean, I know your name and all, but that's about it.'

'Well you won't know me, but I'm Martin McDonald's son. He's a biology lecturer at Bath University.'

'Oh, right. Is he a friend of Bill Sims?'

'They work in the same department.' Joe thought for a moment. 'The thing is, I'm helping him do some research.'

Moreton chuckled and seemed to relax. 'Well good for you, son. In that case – ask away.'

'What he really needs to know is, did anything strange happen while you were in Mexico?'

There was a pause.

'That's kind of a funny question.'

'I know,' said Joe. 'But it would be a big help if you could answer it . . .'

'Matter of fact, there was something strange happened, first time we took the sub down.'

'The sub?'

'Yeah. I'm guessing you know about the programme?'

'No, not really.'

'OK, well that's why we're here, and that's why your guy Sims was here too.'

Joe frowned.

'William Sims was with you?'

'Yeah, Bill was part of the team. We're working with NASA to explore El Zacatón, the world's deepest sinkhole. Trying to find out what kind of life might exist down there. Anyway, because of what happened we had to bring her up again.'

Feeling the pain in his leg returning, Joe winced and transferred his weight to the other foot.

'What did happen?'

'Well, it's kinda hard to explain. None of us could really figure it out. But while the sub was down there, these strange objects came out of nowhere and covered the lights and the cameras. It was the weirdest thing.'

'What did they look like?'

'Hard to say. I mean, you have to understand it was pretty murky down there. But the nearest I can get to it is to say they were kind of . . . wormy lookin'. Hello? Joe? Are ya still there, buddy?'

Joe leaned against the wall and clamped the phone tightly to his ear.

'These worm things – were they still there when you brought the sub up?'

'No,' said Moreton. 'Not a trace of 'em. That was what was so weird. They were all over it in the water, but when we pulled the sub out they'd disappeared.'

'Are you sure?'

'I'm perfectly sure. Why?'

'Because I think William Sims must have brought one of them back with him.'

'That's impossible,' Moreton replied. 'I was with him the whole time.'

'You're not with him now though, are you?'

'No. He had to cut his visit short, apparently. Something came up.'

'Professor Moreton,' said Joe, 'William Sims is dead. He was killed last night at the university.'

There was silence at the other end of the line. Then Moreton asked, 'Is this some kind of a joke?'

'I wish it was,' said Joe. 'But I think Professor Sims was killed by whatever it was he brought back. And now it's starting to attack other people too. Me included.'

'Alright,' said Moreton, his voice suddenly brusque. 'Very funny. But you know what? I'm a busy man, and I really don't have time for this.'

'Wait,' Joe protested, desperate to stop Moreton from hanging up. 'I swear I'm telling the truth. And if you're anywhere near that sinkhole, you need to get as far away from it as you can.'

'Young man,' said Moreton irritably, 'if I were you, I would find better things to do with my time than playing practical jokes on people I don't even know.'

'Damn it!' said Joe as Moreton hung up.

Then he heard the crunch of tyres on gravel and the slamming of car doors.

Suddenly the hallway was full of colour and noise, paramedics in green, police officers in blue and the intermittent crackle of radios.

'Hey!' Joe yelled. 'Shut the door!'

Two police officers – unused to being ordered about by thirteen-year-old boys – stared at him with blank expressions. Joe ran across the hall, slammed the door and leaned back on it.

'Just keep it shut, alright?'

As the others made their way through into the living room, the older of the two policemen saw the look on Joe's face and put a hand on his shoulder. 'Alright, son,' he said. 'Maybe you should come and tell us what's been happening.'

When they reached the living room, Joe saw that it was full of people. In addition to the two uniformed policemen there was a WPC sitting on the sofa next to Linda Barclay, holding her hand while a paramedic bandaged her arm. Another paramedic was dabbing at the side of Giles's head with antiseptic and, over by the French windows, a plain-clothes police officer was staring at a splash of blood on the wall.

But it was the man standing in front of the mantelpiece who drew Joe's attention. He was wearing protective gloves and turning the sword over in his hands, paying particular attention to the streak of blood across the middle of the blade. He wore the same beige chinos and blue shirt that he had worn the last time Joe had seen him. But there was something different about him now. And as he looked up and stared at Joe, trying to recall where he had seen him before, Joe realised what it was.

Sergeant Harris no longer had the look of the tough, crime-hardened detective that Joe had seen at his father's house.

Instead, he looked like a man who was running out of ideas.

Like a man who was scared half to death.

23

Ellis Wood had never liked school. He had never liked the fact that all those stuck-up people in high-street suits and shiny shoes were allowed to get in his face and tell him what to do.

So he had spent the last five years telling them where they could stick their homework, waiting for the day when he could walk out of those school gates for good.

And at last, two months ago, he had done just that. At first it had felt good. He would get up at noon, grab a bowl of cereal and sit watching DVDs for the rest of the day. When his mum came home she would hoover round him and moan that he never did anything to help. Then she'd do him a nice fry-up of fish and chips. And when she had gone to bed, he would nick some money from her purse and go out on the razz with his mates.

But last week, his mum had got wise to him and

started hiding her purse. And when he had asked her to lend him a few quid, she had told him no, she wasn't going to sub him any more and here's an idea, Ellis, why don't you go out and get yourself a job?

So Ellis had gone down to the jobcentre and found himself back with people in high-street suits and shiny shoes, asking him what qualifications he had. When he said none, they sucked air through their teeth, shook their heads and went tappety-tap-tap on their computers. Then they told him that, if he was lucky, he might be able to work in some dung-heap of a burger restaurant for twelve hours a day, shaking fries and asking: 'Do you want ketchup with that?' But he'd get less than four quid an hour for the privilege and would definitely have to smarten himself up because there would be dozens of people after the same job.

So Ellis had told them where they could stick their burgers.

And that was when he had decided to go self-employed.

Which was why, at half past eight on a Saturday night, Ellis Wood was not in the pub with his friends.

He was sitting on a wooden bench by the canal, waiting for his first customer.

* * *

Milton Roberts took one last look at the gleaming surfaces, the spotless examination table and the recently polished floor and decided that he could do no more. He thought about the vegetables he had prepared so carefully before coming to work this morning, laid out on their little chopping board in the fridge. The chilled ranks of parsnip and potato would still be there, quiet and unmoving, waiting for him to come home and turn them into soup. He liked the way that eating these things brought them back to life for a while, the way it made them part of him.

Satisfied that everything was in order, he zipped up his jacket, turned out the lights and closed the door. As he turned the key in the lock and moved from light into shadow, he wondered, *Is this what death is like?*

But Milton did not dwell on such thoughts, because today had been the opposite of death; life had thrown back its dull, heavy curtains and allowed the light of possibility to come streaming in. Doctor Page had asked for his help and now he wanted to shout it from the rooftops:

'Today I am an assistant no longer. Today I am a pathologist!'

But Milton didn't shout from the rooftops. Nor

did he do as he usually did and take the number 28 bus back to his flat on the outskirts of the city. Instead, he did something he hadn't done for a long time. He took a right into Waterside Avenue, crossed the small iron bridge behind the deserted tobacco factory and began to walk home along the path next to the canal. Because, as Doctor Page had observed as he was washing his hands at the end of the post-mortem, 'Life is a delicate thing, Milton. It's here and then it's gone. We have to make the best of it while we can.'

All those years, thought Milton. All those years of sameness, wearing a dull groove of routine between work and home – a bus ride here, a bus ride there, never looking up at the world or noticing what it had to offer.

But now Doctor Page had shown him that there were doors all around him; he just needed the courage to push them open and step through. And as Milton walked along by the canal, breathing the clean air and humming a little tune, he was filled with a fierce, wild joy at the thought that, finally, his life had begun.

Ellis Wood heard the man some time before he saw him. He was humming to himself, quietly and tune-lessly, and Ellis could tell, even from such scant information, that this man was not going to be a problem. He sat upright, took out a cigarette and put it, unlit, in his mouth. Next he took out his pocket knife, placing it on his knee and covering it with his palm. Then he fixed his eyes on the shadows beneath the bridge and waited.

As he walked under the arch of the bridge, Milton saw the boy up ahead and, just for a moment, thought about turning back. There was something about the way he looked at Milton that made him uneasy. But then he remembered something from his school days, something that had helped him survive through all those long, unhappy years:

Don't ever let them see that you're scared.

Milton took a deep breath and continued walking. He kept his eyes on the ragged drifts of grass that grew next to the canal path and the shards of broken light, shining on the water.

'Alright, mate? Got a light?'

Milton stopped, his hands twitching nervously by his sides. He should have taken the bus. If only he'd taken the bus.

'I-I'm sorry. I don't smoke.'

'Very sensible. Smoking's bad for your health.'

Milton smiled weakly. He wasn't good at conversation. He stared at the boy, trying to think of something he could say to make this be over.

'Do you know what else is bad for your health?' asked the boy.

'No,' replied Milton, although this wasn't strictly true. He knew lots of things that were bad for your health. He had seen the results many times, stretched out on the slab in front of him.

But he knew that this was not what the boy wanted to hear.

'Carrying too much money around. That's bad for your health.'

The boy smiled, but it was not a pleasant smile.

'I see,' said Milton. 'Well, I really should be going now.'

'Do you know why carrying too much money around is bad?'

'No I don't,' said Milton unhappily.

'Because the world is full of people who want to take it off you.'

'Oh,' said Milton.

'Yes,' said the boy. '*Oh*.'

'I really should be getting back now,' said Milton.

The boy, who had been standing by the bench, now stepped in front of Milton and blocked his path.

'Have *you* got any money?' he asked.

Milton thought of the small, zipped leather purse

that his mother had given him for his birthday. It was such a thoughtful gift. So typical of her.

'No,' he said. 'Not much.'

He had £17.50, enough for his bus fare and some groceries from the corner shop. But he wouldn't get paid again until next week. And he didn't want to give his purse away.

The boy stepped closer.

'But you said you don't smoke.'

'I don't.'

'Do you know how much a packet of cigarettes costs?'

'No.'

'Over five quid. So by not smoking, you'll have saved a fortune. Whereas, because I smoke, I have no money. It's not fair, is it?'

Milton shrugged. He was thoroughly miserable now. He wanted to be safe at home, cooking his vegetable soup. He sighed and pictured all the ingredients in the fridge, waiting for him to come home and work his magic.

'I said, it's not fair, is it?'

It *was* fair, of course. Milton knew that. If this boy chose to spend his money on cigarettes, then that was his lookout. But Milton also knew that fairness was not what this conversation was about.

'Please,' he said. 'I want to go home now.'

'Nuh-uh,' said the boy, holding up his hand to stop Milton as he tried to walk past. 'Not so fast.'

Milton stopped. He glanced over the boy's shoulder at the wooden fence that separated the canal from the road. He thought about trying to run. But then he looked at the boy's rough, sinewy fists and decided against it.

'How about we make life a bit fairer?'

'What do you mean?' asked Milton.

'You give me some money, and then we've both got some. That makes it fair, doesn't it?'

'No,' said Milton. 'It doesn't.'

He felt as if he was ten years old again, cowering in the playground as the bigger boys beat him and took his dinner money away.

'Well I think it does.'

The boy raised his right hand and, as Milton watched, he folded his fingers down to reveal the bright silver blade of a knife.

'Come on,' he said, all pretence of politeness gone. 'Give me your money.'

Milton thought of Doctor Page then, washing his hands and saying, *Life is a delicate thing, Milton. It's here and then it's gone.* He thought of the body, cold on the slab. And his heart cried out because so many bright doorways were suddenly closing – all except one – and there was no light, and he did not want to walk through it.

So Milton did the only thing he could think of.

He put his head down and ran.

Ellis Wood guessed that the man would try to make a break for it, but when it happened it was so fast that it almost caught him off guard.

Almost, but not quite.

As the man thumped past his shoulder, Ellis stuck his leg out and watched him sprawl across the path in a tumble of dust.

'Leave me alone!' squeaked the man in a small, frightened voice. He scrabbled to his feet and tried to run, but Ellis grabbed his jumper and pulled him backwards. Hooking an arm around his neck, he held the knife in front of him so that the man could see it glint in the fading light. Ellis tightened his grip and put his lips close to the man's ear.

'Give me the money,' he whispered, 'and then you can go.'

In all the forty-six years of his life, Milton had never been so scared. Not when he had laid out his first body, nor when his father had beaten him for having mud on his shoes; not even when the boys in the playground had punched him sobbing to the ground. Milton had been afraid on each of these occasions, but each time he had told himself, *I will survive.*

This time he was not so sure.

'Stop!' he pleaded, reaching into the pocket of his jacket. 'Just let go and I'll get it.'

The boy relaxed his grip, but as Milton's fingers closed around the soft leather of the purse, the boy suddenly screamed and pulled away. And as Milton braced himself for the sharp strike of the knife between his shoulder blades, the boy began to shriek, loudly, as though *he* was the one being attacked. Confused, Milton turned round to see the knife lying on the path and the boy on the ground next to it, rolling around and punching at the grass.

This was his chance.

If he ran now, Milton knew he would be safe.

But as he turned to make his escape, the boy cried out – not just an ordinary cry, but the terrified scream of someone who believes they are about to die.

Turning back once more, Milton was confronted by the sight of a large snake-like creature gripping the boy's leg, thrashing its tail back and forth as it tore at the muscle beneath his jeans. As Milton watched, the boy clawed at the ground and turned his face to look at him.

'Help me!' he screamed. 'Please! You've got to

help me!'

Every instinct told Milton to run away as fast as he could. Why should he help someone who had tried to hurt him? But then the boy cried out again and suddenly Milton knew that, whatever he had done, this young boy did not belong on a slab; the molecules that made him had not come together only to be torn back into stillness by this hideous, writhing monstrosity.

So Milton didn't run. Instead, he did the bravest thing he had ever done in his life: he picked up the knife and sprinted towards the boy and his attacker. When the boy saw Milton with the knife he cried out again and raised an arm to protect himself. But Milton had no intention of attacking him. Instead he kicked the monstrous creature as hard as he could and, as it reared up to reveal a gaping circle of teeth, he thrust his arm forward and buried the knife deep into its side.

'Run!' he shouted as the creature fell sideways, jerking and twitching across the grass. 'Run!'

Grabbing the boy's arm, Milton pulled him to his feet and dragged him along the path. 'Come on!' he urged. 'We have to get out of here!' Hearing a rustle of movement in the grass behind them, he put his hand in the centre of the boy's back and pushed just as the bushes erupted and something thumped against Milton's shoulder. There was a sharp, tearing pain and Milton cried out, but he kept on moving. 'Go over!' he shouted. 'Over the fence!'

As the boy climbed over, Milton ripped the squirming, slimy mass from his shoulder, placed both hands on top of the fence and vaulted over, catching his foot on the top. He landed head first in a patch of stinging nettles before rolling down the steep verge into the road. A car swerved, hooted and then accelerated away, its tyres squealing smoke and rubber. Milton staggered back towards the pavement and sat on the kerb. He touched his shoulder and saw that his fingers were wet with blood.

'Hey mate,' said a voice. 'Are you OK?'

Milton glanced up to see the boy standing above him. His hands were shaking and his face was white with shock.

'Yes,' replied Milton, staring at a rainbow of oil in the road. 'I think so.'

'Listen . . . I just wanted to say thanks, you know. For getting that thing off me and everything.'

'You're welcome,' replied Milton politely, surprised by his own lack of anger.

'I mean, what was it? What the hell was that thing?' The boy rubbed his leg and glanced up at the fence, afraid that the creature might suddenly come squirming over the top of it. 'Do you think it's gone?'

Milton shrugged. 'I don't know,' he said. 'But I don't think we should stay around to find out.'

He took out his purse, unzipped it and pulled out a five-pound note.

'Here,' he said. 'You could probably use some cigarettes.'

The boy nodded and took the money almost apologetically.

'Thanks. You're a good man.'

After he had gone, Milton Roberts sat on the grass verge and thought about that. Then, aware of the increasing pain in his shoulder, he tentatively pulled back his jacket and examined the wound.

'Well I never,' he whispered, staring at the strange, distinctive pattern that marked his flesh. 'Well I never did.'

He stood up and took one last look at the fence and the flattened nettles beside it. Then he hurried away down the street, anxious to telephone Doctor Page with this latest and most remarkable news.

24

The world was crazy and getting crazier; suddenly everything seemed to be moving at a hundred miles an hour. As Joe sat in the back of the police car listening to the sirens wail he nudged Giles and whispered, 'You know what? I think we might be getting somewhere.'

The driver kept his foot down but Sergeant Harris, who had been listening, hooked an arm around the headrest and peered through the gap between the seats.

'Getting your stories straight?' he asked, and Joe saw that he was worried. The world had stopped making sense and Sergeant Harris didn't like it one little bit.

'We don't need to get our stories straight,' said Joe, 'because we're telling the truth.'

For a moment Harris didn't seem to know what to say. As they wove in and out of the traffic he scratched at the stubble on his chin and stared out of the window at the houses and shop fronts as they slid past in a blur of light.

'You must understand,' he said at last, 'that what you have told me is so absurd, so ridiculous, that I would have to be the world's biggest fool to believe it.'

Joe was about to protest, but Harris held up a hand to quieten him.

'As crazy as your story may be, however, you're not the first ones to tell me it. So I'm thinking there are two possible explanations. First, that there's some kind of weird conspiracy to protect the person responsible for these deaths.'

'And the second?' asked Giles.

'The second,' replied Harris, 'is that you may just be telling the truth.'

Joe glanced at Giles, then back at Harris.

'Which one are you going for?' he asked.

Harris ran his hand through what remained of his hair and sighed.

'The second one,' he said. 'But if I'm right, then God help us all.'

The sharp sting of Joe's injuries had blurred into a general ache all over his body. It had been a long day and he felt exhausted – not just physically, but mentally too. As Giles was taken off by another police officer, Joe followed Harris down a neon-lit corridor and felt light-headed, disconnected from the world, as though he were sleepwalking through some kind of a dream. The clanging doors and echoing foot-steps seemed to come from a place far away, some-where that had nothing to do with him.

When they reached the end of the corridor, Harris pushed open a door and Joe's heart beat faster as he recognised the small table and the cam-era on the wall. It was the room in which he had last seen his father.

'Alright, Joe,' said Harris. 'Superintendent Reeve is going to join us in a minute, and I want you to tell him exactly what you told me, OK?'

Joe sat down, blinking in the harsh light.

'Where's Giles?'

'He's talking with another officer just now.'

'To make sure we get our stories straight?'

Harris gave him a half smile. 'Something like that.'

The door opened and a tall, wiry man with silver crowns sewn onto the shoulders of his jacket walked in. Behind him was a plain-clothes officer whom Joe didn't recognise and Susie from the Child Protection Team, whom he did.

'Hello, Joe,' she said. 'How are things?'

Joe looked at her. 'Well, you know. They've been better.'

Susie smiled sympathetically and put a hand on his shoulder.

'Superintendent Reeve just wants to hear what happened,' she explained. 'Superintendent, this is Joe McDonald – Martin McDonald's son.'

The tall man looked at Joe. 'Well then. Perhaps you'd like to tell me what you know?'

'OK,' said Joe. 'But I'm not sure you're going to believe it.'

When Joe had finished, Superintendent Reeve shook his head and looked at Harris incredulously.

'You seriously expect me to believe this, Sergeant Harris?'

'I know it sounds crazy, sir,' said Harris. 'But I presume you've heard about Rose Gardens?'

'I know that an old lady was attacked there, yes. I also know her daughter is being treated as a suspect.'

'Well, the thing is, I spoke to the daughter and she gave me the same story. About being attacked by some weird snake-like creature.'

'But she doesn't live anywhere near the canal.'

'I know. Apparently it came out of the toilet.'

Reeve stared at Harris as if he had taken leave of

his senses.

'The *toilet*?'

'I know, I know. But get this: there was blood in the toilet bowl, same as there was at the lab where we found Sims.'

There was silence as Harris finished speaking and Reeve stared at him in amazement.

'Has anyone actually *seen* one of these creatures?'

'I have,' said Joe.

'Anyone else?' said Reeve, looking pointedly at Harris.

'No,' said Harris, 'but if you think about it for a minute–'

'I *am* thinking about it,' Reeve interrupted, 'and what I'm thinking is, I have never heard anything so ridiculous in all my life.'

'But–'

'Listen, Sergeant. I know we're all desperate to get these cases cleared up. I've got the local paper practically kicking my door down trying to get answers from me. But coming up with some half-baked fairy-tale about giant serpents is not going to help anyone, is it?'

'But, sir, from what we know–'

'Sergeant Harris, I think we have already established that what you know can probably be written on the back of a postage stamp. Now if you'll excuse me, I have work to do.'

As he turned to go, the door opened and Joe recognised the uniformed sergeant from the reception desk. He held a phone in one hand and, when he saw the superintendent, he held it out to him.

'Sorry to interrupt, sir,' he said, 'but it's Doctor Page.'

Reeve scowled.

'Can't it wait?'

The desk sergeant covered the mouthpiece with his hand.

'He says it's urgent.'

'Alright. Give it to me.'

Reeve took the phone and held it to his ear. As he listened, Joe saw a change come over him. His face – which had been an angry red during his exchange with Harris – began to lose its colour and his lips pressed together into a thin, bloodless line.

'Are you sure?' Reeve asked. 'What time was this?'

Joe studied his expression, trying to work out what the conversation might be about.

'No, I understand,' Reeve said. 'Are you able to come to the station?' A pause. 'In the next ten minutes would be good.' He finished the call and stared at the handset.

'That was the pathologist,' he said quietly. 'One of his assistants was attacked on his way home this evening. Apparently he noticed that his wounds were of a similar pattern to those found on the body of William Sims, so he contacted Doctor Page. Page examined him and discovered that this was indeed the case.'

'Can the assistant identify who attacked him?' asked Susie.

'Not who,' said Reeve. '*What.*'

He turned to Joe.

'You're telling the truth, aren't you, son?'

Joe nodded.

'Then I want you to tell me something. And I need you to think carefully, because this is important. What time was it when you were first attacked?'

'I, I'm not sure. We'd just passed a fisherman with a radio. The football was about to kick off.'

Reeve looked at his watch.

'So around three p.m., something like that?'

'Sounds about right.'

'Which is around the same time that Maureen Lewis's neighbour reported hearing strange noises coming from her house.'

'Meaning?' said Harris.

'Meaning that either this thing can move incredibly fast, or–'

'Or there's more than one of them,' said Joe.

'Exactly,' said Reeve. 'And if that's true, we need to get that whole stretch of canal checked out fast.'

'And not just the canal,' said Harris. 'That thing came up through the waste pipe into the bathroom in Rose Gardens, same way as it left the university lab. Whatever it is, it's learned to navigate the sewage system.'

'So what is it?' asked Reeve. 'What exactly are we dealing with here?'

'I have no idea,' said Harris.

'I know someone who might be able to help,' said Joe.

Everyone turned to look at him at once.

'Who?' asked Reeve.

'My dad,' said Joe.

25

'I don't understand,' said Martin McDonald as he was brought into the room. 'What's going on?'

It felt strange for Joe in those few seconds, watching his father without him realising that he was there. He looked tired; there were dark rings beneath his eyes and a sprinkling of dark stubble peppered his chin. But Joe didn't care about that. All he cared about was that he was seeing him again.

'Hi, Dad,' he said. 'How's it going?'

'Joe?' As Martin McDonald's eyes fell upon the small figure sitting at the table, he looked at the bruised face and the torn, bloodstained clothes and his mouth fell open. 'Joe, what happened to you?'

'It's a bit of a long story,' said Joe. 'But they know, Dad. They know it's not you.'

Martin McDonald stared at Harris, a look of disbelief on his face.

'Is this true?'

Harris nodded. 'Yes, Mr McDonald,' he said, loosening his collar. 'As the duty sergeant is currently explaining to your solicitor, it seems that we may have been a little hasty. When we first brought you in, the evidence we had appeared to be fairly conclusive. But there have since been . . .' here he paused and cleared his throat '. . . new developments.'

Joe's dad looked from Harris to Reeve.

'Will somebody please tell me what is going on?'

'The thing that killed Professor Sims,' said Joe, 'tried to kill some other people. And it tried to kill me too.'

'What?' Joe's dad pulled the chair from under the table and sat down. 'What do you mean?'

'I spoke to Professor Moreton, like you asked. He's in Mexico. He said something about lowering a sub into a sinkhole and talked about these strange worm-like creatures that they'd seen. I asked him if Professor Sims could have brought one back with him, but he said no because when the sub surfaced they'd all disappeared. And when I told him they were attacking people over here and that Professor Sims had been killed, he didn't believe me and hung up. But I'm sure that's what they are.'

'Wait,' said Reeve, 'A sinkhole? Mexico? You never mentioned any of this before.'

Joe shrugged. 'That's all I know.'

'Are you sure about this?' asked Joe's dad. 'Are these things really attacking people?'

Harris nodded. 'It would seem so, yes.'

'I told him,' said Joe's dad, shaking his head. 'First time I saw it, I knew it was dangerous. I warned him not to mess with things he didn't understand.'

Reeve stepped forward. 'Are you saying you knew about this too, Mr McDonald?' he asked.

'Not exactly. I mean, I knew Bill had something strange and I knew he shouldn't have brought it back with him. But I had no idea it had anything to do with what happened to him. That's why I didn't tell you about it.'

'But you just said you thought these things were dangerous. How could you possibly know?'

'I didn't at first. When I got to the lab I was surprised to find Bill there since he wasn't due back for another week. He told me he'd had to come back early, but didn't say why. He seemed pretty restless, unable to settle. And he kept looking over at this tank in the corner.

'Tank?' asked Harris.

'Yes. An aquarium.'

'How big?'

'About so big.' Joe's dad used his hands to frame a space the size of a small fish tank. 'Why?'

'Because we found the remains of a tank about

that size at the scene,' replied Harris.

Joe's dad nodded. 'Makes sense. But did you find what was in it?'

'No.' Harris shook his head. 'What *was* in it?'

'I don't know exactly. First of all I thought it was a leech or something. But when I looked more closely, I saw that it wasn't like anything I'd ever seen before. It was green and slimy, about the size of my middle finger. And as it moved through the water it kept moving its head around, as if it was searching for something.'

Joe frowned. 'The thing that attacked me was much bigger than that,' he said.

'Hmm,' said Reeve. 'Maybe we're talking about two different things.'

'Not necessarily,' said Joe's dad. 'Bill told me that when he first found it, it was easily small enough to fit inside a test tube.'

'That would explain the words on the paper,' said Harris.

'What words?' asked Reeve.

Harris took out his notebook and flicked back through the pages.

'*Rapid growth rate. High mobility. Intelligent.* They were written on a notepad we found on the table.'

Reeve looked at Joe's dad. 'So you're saying this thing had already grown a lot by the time you saw it?'

'From what Bill told me, yes. Its growth rate was faster than anything he'd ever seen. He was very excited about it. But I remember, while he was telling me about it, something very strange happened.'

'What kind of strange?'

'While he was talking I was watching it out of the corner of my eye. It was moving all the time, flowing through the water, and as it got nearer to the wall of the tank, I crouched down to get a better look. At the same moment it flung itself hard against the glass, splashing water out through the lid. It was quite a shock, I can tell you. Bill said he'd never seen it do anything like that before. But it seemed extremely aggressive. Predatory even. As if it was trying to get at me.'

Harris put away his notebook and stood by the table, hands in his pockets.

'So what did you two argue about?'

Joe's dad shrugged.

'Well, for one thing, bringing something like this out of its natural environment without the agreement of the relevant authorities is a big no-no. It's professional misconduct of the highest order. If anyone found out about it, it would severely damage the department's reputation.'

'That's it? That's why you had the argument?'

'Partly. But also because I spend my life lecturing on the natural balance of the world. About how human interference can mess it up. If you bring something out of its natural habitat and place it in a new one, there are two possibilities.'

'Which are?'

'Either it will live, or it will die. If it dies, then the chances are that you may just have killed off one of the last remaining specimens of its kind. But if it lives and thrives, then it has the potential to upset the balance of its new habitat.'

Reeve frowned. 'So you think that's what's happening?'

Joe's dad shook his head. 'From what you say, I'm afraid it may be a lot more serious than that. I'm starting to think that it might actually be something scientists have been warning about for years: a kind of growth-limiting factor for the human race.'

'What do you mean?' asked Reeve.

'I mean,' said Joe's dad, 'that I think it probably wants to kill as many of us as it can.'

26

It was after midnight. The meeting room was packed with police officers and Joe could tell by the way some of them were rubbing their eyes that they must have been called in at short notice. A group of eight men on one side of the room were dressed differently from the others: they wore heavy boots together with dark blue canvas trousers, flak jackets and blue chequered caps. Each one carried a small sub-machine gun with a torch fitted beneath the barrel.

'Who are they?' Joe whispered.

'Some kind of armed response team,' said his dad. 'They're obviously taking this pretty seriously.'

'About time,' said Joe. Until now he had been feeling desperately tired, but the sudden burst of activity had woken him up again. Watching the men check and recheck their weapons, he felt a thrill of excitement.

'How's it going?' asked a voice behind him.

Joe turned to see Giles pulling up a chair.

'Hey, Giles!' he said. 'What happened? Did they give you a hard time?'

'Not really,' said Giles. 'I was telling them what I'd seen when they found out that some other people had been attacked. They got pretty excited after that.'

The room fell silent as Superintendent Reeve walked to the front.

'Alright, everyone,' he said. 'We don't have much time. I'm sure some of you must be wondering why you've been called in here and the reason is simple: we are dealing with a matter of national security. I have informed Her Majesty's Government of recent events and their emergency committee will be meeting in Whitehall shortly to discuss the situation. In the meantime, it is up to us to do what we can.'

Reeve glanced at the clock on the wall. Then he looked back at the officers in front of him, checking that everyone was listening.

Everyone was.

'Before I go into details, it goes without saying that no individual should speak to the media about any of this. Until such time as the proper facts can be established, all enquiries should be directed straight to me.'

There was an excited buzz around the room and Reeve held up his hands for quiet.

'The situation is this. Over the past twenty-four hours there have been several vicious attacks on members of the public. There has been at least one death and, given the nature and frequency of the attacks, there is a high probability that there will be more. Our enquiries have so far led us to believe that these attacks have been carried out by an aggressive new species of animal from South America, accidentally released into the wild less than two days ago.'

A uniformed officer put up a hand.

'Yes, PC Wallace?'

Wallace lowered his hand again. 'Sir, what kind of animal are we dealing with?'

'Well, I haven't seen it myself,' said Reeve, 'but all reports so far identify it as some kind of serpent or snake-like creature. But, as you might guess, we're not talking about your common or garden water snake here. By all accounts, this animal is over a metre in length and moves extremely rapidly. Evidence suggests it can live both in and out of water, although water appears to be its preferred habitat.'

One of the men dressed in dark combats raised a

hand and Reeve nodded in his direction. 'Yes, Sergeant Lee?'

'How many are we talking about?'

'At the moment, we just don't know. But at this point I'm going to ask Mr McDonald if he'll fill you in on a few of the details. Mr McDonald is a lecturer in environmental biology, so he should know what he's talking about. Is that alright, Mr McDonald?'

'That's fine.'

As his dad stood up and walked to the front, Joe noticed the surprise on a few faces and realised that some of them must have been there earlier when he had been brought in as a murder suspect.

One way or another, it was turning out to be a strange day for everyone.

'A few days ago,' his dad began, 'my colleague Bill Sims was in Mexico, taking part in a programme sponsored by NASA and the US government. The aim of the programme was to test a deep-water submarine by exploring El Zacatón, the world's deepest sinkhole. Bill was excited by the idea that they might find evidence of simple organisms living at such depths which had never been studied before. But as it turned out, he discovered an organism that was far more complex than he ever imagined.'

As Joe watched his father hold the room spell-bound with his quiet confidence, he began to feel that maybe things were heading in the right direction at last.

'Bill's mistake was to bring this creature back with him,' his father continued, 'and I'll tell you why. That environment, deep beneath the earth, has effectively been sealed off from the rest of the world for millions of years. Until now, it has remained virtually unaffected by human activity. But like the bloodstream of the body, if something new appears, like a bacteria or a virus, something that threatens the body's existence, the blood cells will attack it. Once it has been identified as a threat, the cells will multiply. Each new cell will carry the memory of the threat so that whenever they encounter it, they are programmed to attack and kill it. And they will keep on attacking, and they will keep on killing. And they won't stop until the threat is wiped out.'

Joe's dad paused for a moment to let his words sink in.

'I am afraid,' he went on, 'that Bill Sims was simply the first threat. The first virus, if you like. My guess is that this thing is multiplying furiously because it has perceived that it is surrounded by a threat – by a world full of creatures just like Bill Sims. This species feels threatened by you, me and every person on the planet. And it will do anything it can to protect itself. The truth is, we may be looking at the biggest danger to our existence that humanity has ever faced.'

As Joe's dad finished speaking there was stunned silence in the room. Men who only minutes earlier had been laughing and joking were now ashen faced as they thought about the implications of what they had heard.

'So you see,' said Superintendent Reeve, taking his place once more at the front of the room. 'We have no time to lose. I have already instructed traffic units to set up roadblocks around the canal area, where we believe the majority of the creatures are located. The objective of this operation is simple: to actively seek out these vermin and destroy them. Sniffer dogs and armoured frogmen will be on hand to help track them down, but the chances are you won't need to look very hard. Because if Mr McDonald's theory is correct, these things are going to come looking for you.'

As the meeting broke up, Joe turned to Giles.

'I'm sorry about all this,' he said. 'If I hadn't come over to see you, you wouldn't be in this mess right now.'

'Mess?' said Giles. 'Listen, Joe. If it wasn't for you, I'd be stuck inside listening to this on the news. I wouldn't have missed it for the world.'

'But what about your mum?' asked Joe. 'How's

she doing?'

'They took her to the hospital. She's a bit torn up, but the doctors say she's going to be OK. So things could be a lot worse.'

Joe felt a hand on his shoulder and looked up to see his father standing there.

'Hi, Joe,' he said. 'How are you feeling?'

'Bit rough,' said Joe. 'But not bad, considering.'

The pain in his leg had now settled into a dull, bruising ache which he did his best to ignore.

'Well listen. Superintendent Reeve has asked me if you'd be willing to show them the exact place where you were attacked. I told him you'd been through enough, but–'

'I'll do it,' said Joe quickly.

'What?'

'I said I'll do it.'

Secretly Joe was terrified at the possibility of seeing the creatures again. But at the same time, he felt strangely excited. He knew he couldn't stop now. Not until this whole thing was finally over.

'Joe, you don't have to do this,' his dad told him. 'You really don't.'

'I know,' Joe replied. 'But I want to.'

Giles smiled.

'That makes two of us,' he said.

27

Long before they reached the canal, Joe could hear the wail of sirens and see the clusters of blue lights flashing across the city. As they approached Fore Street, two uniformed officers waved them through and the police driver accelerated past a row of parked cars before dabbing at the brakes and turning into Canal Road, tyres squealing in protest. At the end of the street they came to a halt by the small wooden gate that led to the canal and Joe turned to see a ribbon of blue lights flashing behind them.

Suddenly the air was alive with the sound of doors slamming and voices shouting orders.

'OK, lads,' said Sergeant Harris as police officers began disembarking from several vans which had pulled up next to them. 'The armed response team's going in first and we're going right in behind them. But as soon as you've shown us the location, that's your job done and you're straight back in the van.

OK?'

Joe and Giles nodded.

'Sure. No problem.'

'Happy with that, Mr McDonald?'

'Happy as I'm going to be. But I'm coming too.'

As the gate shut behind them, Joe watched the silhouettes of armed officers spread out along the towpath. Beams of torchlight swept across the water and flickered across the tangle of weeds on the far side of the canal.

'It was down there,' whispered Giles, pointing left. 'Down past the bench.'

'Are you sure?' asked Harris.

'Definitely,' said Joe.

'Don't forget that these creatures are extremely mobile,' said Joe's dad. 'They could be anywhere.'

'Maybe,' Harris replied, 'but we have to start somewhere.' He turned to one of the armed officers. 'We'll go left,' he said. 'You take your section right, see what you can find.'

He tapped Joe's dad on the arm. 'If it's alright with you, I'd like the boys to take us as near as they can to where it happened. But don't worry. If those things so much as stick their heads up, we'll blast them all the way to kingdom come.'

Joe looked out across the water and imagined

dark shapes moving silently through the depths towards them.

'Are you two alright with that?' asked Joe's dad.

'Sure,' said Giles.

Joe put his hands in his pockets so that no one would see they were shaking. 'No problem,' he said.

As they walked further down the path he caught the scent of honeysuckle and thought how strange it was that something beautiful could exist in a place where death was so near.

'Is this where you meant?' asked Harris.

Joe looked at the wooden bench where they had sat that afternoon.

'Yeah,' he said. 'This is it.'

Harris took a radio from his pocket and Joe heard the hiss of static. 'This is Harris. You can bring the dogs up now.'

'Are we done?' asked Joe's dad.

'Yeah, we're done.' Harris stepped back to let them pass. 'Listen, thanks for your help on this one. And, you know . . . sorry about the other stuff.'

Joe's dad shrugged. 'That's alright. Just make sure you get it right this time, OK?'

As they walked back along the towpath Giles asked, 'Can't we watch for a while? I wouldn't mind seeing those things get what's coming to them.'

Joe's dad shook his head. 'It's too dangerous,' he

said. 'If the bullets start flying there's no knowing where they'll end up.'

'Shame,' said Giles. 'Sounds like I'll have to watch it on TV after all.'

But as they neared the gate, Joe's dad stopped.

'Listen. Did you hear that?'

They listened, but all Joe could hear was the sound of approaching sirens.

'I can't hear anything,' he said.

'I'm sure I heard something in the water,' said Joe's dad. Stepping off the towpath, he walked across the grassy strip that bordered the canal.

'Dad,' said Joe nervously as his father stared out across the water. 'Don't. Please. Come on. Let's go back to the van.'

'In a minute,' said his dad, taking another step towards the water's edge. 'I just want to take a look.'

'Joe's right, Mr McDonald,' said Giles. 'Seriously. You don't want to mess with those things.'

Joe's dad stared at the water for a few more seconds, then shrugged and turned back. 'I must have imagined it,' he said. 'I guess I just really wanted to see one for myself.'

'Trust me,' said Giles. 'You really don't.'

Joe's leg was hurting now. All he wanted was to be back home, lying in a warm, comfortable bed. He wanted to sleep, to forget the day and wake up to find that his life was back to normal once more.

As he watched his dad turn away from the canal, he breathed a sigh of relief.

And that was when the water exploded.

28

It happened so fast that Joe didn't even have time to shout a warning. As the water erupted, a dark shape shot past them, twisted through the air and hit Joe's dad in the side of the face, lifting him clean off the ground. For a split second he was airborne, then with a splash he hit the water and disappeared.

'Dad!' Joe screamed. 'Dad!'

Giles swore and began running up the canal path shouting for help, but Joe was already at the water's edge, scanning the surface for some sign that his father was still alive. He stared at the ripples spreading out across the water. 'No,' he whispered. 'No, no, *no* . . .'

Then he took a deep breath and jumped.

The shock of hitting the cold water made him gasp, but he kicked off his shoes and dived beneath the surface, his muscles tightening like wet ropes beneath his skin.

Shivering, he opened his eyes and tried to peer into the gloom. But the water was dark and all he could see were patterns of moonlight, fading from blue to black. As he reached out into the freezing dark his lungs cried out for oxygen. He swam to the surface, splashing up into the warm sweet air and gulping it down.

'Joe!' Giles yelled from the bank. 'Swim back! Swim back!'

For a moment Joe was tempted, imagining the creature moving towards him beneath the surface. But he knew that somewhere down there his father was drowning. There was no one else who would save him.

Taking another deep breath, he flipped over and swam down again. Weeds brushed his cheeks as he slid into the blackness.

Please, he thought. *Let me find what I am searching for.*

Suddenly, unexpectedly, he caught sight of his father. He was just beneath the surface, his face pale and milky against the weeds. As Joe swam closer he saw that the serpent was wrapped around his body, twisting, squirming and snapping at his throat.

Pulling his arms back, Joe swam towards his father until their faces were almost touching. Clenching his fist, he punched the squirming creature, but it didn't move and seconds later he saw his father go limp. For a moment, it seemed to Joe as if the world had won. But then a spark of anger flashed inside him and he grabbed the creature's head, sunk his nails in hard and pulled.

The powerful serpent released its grip and a cloud of blood ballooned from its mouth. It began thrashing about in his hands, but he held on with all his strength and kicked his way up to the surface. As he broke through there was a loud splash and suddenly Giles was next to him, shouting and yelling and pummelling the creature with both fists. As they floundered together in the water, there was a flash of torchlight and Joe saw that the men on the bank were aiming their guns.

'Swim away, Giles!' he shouted, using the last of his strength to push the creature's head out of the water. 'Swim away!' For a second the serpent's eyes glowed red in the darkness. Then there was a crackle of gunfire and the top of its body disappeared in a meaty blur of blood and skin, chunks of flesh pattering down across the surface of the water.

Joe turned to see his father floating face down, arms outstretched as if embracing the darkness below.

'Giles! Help me get him to the side!' he shouted, swimming desperately towards his father. Together they propelled him towards the bank, where strong hands were waiting to pull him up onto the towpath.

Joe levered himself out of the canal and collapsed next to Giles. The cold water soaked his skin as he lay gasping in the sweet-smelling grass. Along the canal he could hear the snap of ammunition being loaded into magazines and the metallic ring of spent cartridges bouncing across the path. He turned his head and saw his father on his hands and knees, coughing up water.

'Thank God,' he breathed. 'Thank God.'

Powerful torch beams swept the surface of the canal as police marksmen searched for reasons to pull their triggers.

'Keep your eyes on the water!' someone shouted. Harris paced up and down the path, phone clamped to his ear.

'Yeah we got one,' he said. 'We're waiting to see if any others are going to show.' He paced some more, listening. 'No, no sign of any others.' Another pause, then: 'Hang on, I'll ask him.'

He looked across at Joe's dad, who was slumped against the bench, trying to get his breath back.

'Mr McDonald, do you think this area is safe now?'

Joe watched his father press his palms against his

eyes, wipe away the water and then slowly shake his head.

'No,' he said, 'I don't.'

Harris chewed his lip. He frowned.

'Why not?'

'Because,' said Joe's dad, 'I saw another one down there.'

Joe looked at Harris and saw that this was not the answer he had been hoping for.

Harris put the phone back against his ear.

'We have another possible sighting, so we're remaining on high alert. Depends how things go, but we might have to call in the army. Yeah, OK. Will do.'

As Harris snapped the phone shut, Sergeant Lee pushed through the gate with a fresh detachment of armed police behind him.

'You missed all the fun,' said Harris. 'Any news on the helicopter?'

'On its way,' said Lee. Joe looked up and saw a silver light in the sky, growing gradually bigger as it moved towards them.

'Oh well,' said Harris. 'Better late than never.' He walked across to a young uniformed officer and tapped him on the shoulder. 'Got a job for you, Constable,' he said. Joe recognised him as the young policeman who had been on duty outside his house.

'I need this lot taken out of harm's way. Take them over to the hospital and get them checked out, will you?'

Joe saw the disappointment on the young officer's face and guessed this was probably the most exciting thing that had ever happened to him. Now he was going to miss seeing the end of it. As the officer walked towards them, Joe realised he was going to miss it too. But he was going somewhere warm and safe, and that was definitely worth the trade-off.

Stepping back to let a couple of dog handlers through, he turned to follow the others. Behind him he could hear Harris barking orders into his phone.

'We need more divers,' he was saying. 'I want to make absolutely certain this section is clear.'

As the gate banged shut behind him, Joe turned for a last look at the place where his life had almost ended. In the glare of the searchlight he saw a dog handler by the water's edge, pulling back on the leash as the dog strained against it.

The dog barked twice.

Then the water boiled, turned black and a living torrent of darkness rose up, seething over the grass towards them like a tidal wave from hell.

'Get back!' screamed Harris, waving an arm frantically at his men as they began firing into the dark mass which was moving rapidly across the grass towards them.

Joe froze, open-mouthed, unable to believe the scene that was unfolding in front of him. As the police dog and its handler disappeared beneath the wave of writhing creatures, one of the armed response team opened fire with his machine gun and three of the serpents split and blurred like strawberries in a blender. But as he staggered backwards, still firing, the creatures swept over him, ripping at his flesh in a twitching, squirming frenzy.

Joe saw another dog handler disappear beneath the relentless onslaught, his wild-eyed Alsatian snapping at the creatures as they foamed over it, dragging it yelping to the ground. As individual police officers fell, the tide of creatures split and swarmed around them, drawn to them like iron filings to magnets. Giles punched Joe's arm and pointed to the guns that lay scattered on the grass, dropped by their injured owners.

'Come on!' he shouted. 'They need our help!'

Then he was gone and suddenly Joe was jumping the gate and running across the grass after him. He heard his dad shout, 'Joe, come back!' somewhere behind him but he kept on running, the crackle of gunfire echoing through the still night air. Dark clusters of creatures writhed all around him and he knew that, somewhere beneath them, people were dying.

'Here!' shouted Giles, grabbing one of the guns. 'Fire short bursts and aim high – make sure you don't hit the guys underneath.' He threw one gun to Joe, then picked another and pointed it at the nearest cluster. He squeezed off a couple of bursts and the serpents blew apart in a spray of red mist, revealing the bloodied face of an officer beneath.

As Giles fired again, Joe squinted down the barrel of his own weapon and pulled the trigger. His first shots went wide, kicking up clods of earth on the far side of the canal, but he lowered the gun slightly and fired three more times in quick succession. This time his aim was true and the cluster bloomed scarlet, peeling open to reveal a ragged, broken body beneath.

As Joe took aim at a group by the water's edge he noticed two serpents slithering across the grass towards Giles. Bumping him sideways with his shoulder, Joe squinted down the gun barrel and fired. The first volley went high, whining off across the water, but the second struck the nearest creature low in the body, flipping it up into the air and sending it cartwheeling across the grass. Seeing the second serpent lunge at Giles's leg, Joe pulled the trigger again and the weapon kicked back into his shoulder. The creature dissolved into tattered ribbons in front of him, the impact of the bullets flinging it backward in a spray of red.

As Giles recovered and shot two more from the nearest group Joe felt his stomach begin to heave, but he swallowed and took aim at a third cluster close to the canal.

'That's it, lads, keep going!' shouted a voice next to him.

Joe turned to see Harris picking up another gun and slamming a fresh magazine into the stock. Next to him stood the young policeman and Joe's dad, both of them firing at a group of serpents that were tearing at the legs of a fallen officer. The creatures jumped and twitched as the bullets slammed into them, falling back and becoming entangled with one another as they tried to twist away from this latest attack.

Joe turned his attention back to the cluster by the canal, but as he pulled the trigger there was a metallic click and he realised he was out of ammo. Looking around for a fresh magazine, he spotted a machine gun down by the water's edge. Although there were two clusters between him and the gun, the first had been torn apart by gunfire and the second was dissolving in a hail of bullets as he watched, jumping and popping like a bunch of ketchup-filled balloons.

'Giles!' he shouted. 'Watch my back, OK?'

Dropping his weapon he ran, following a straight path between the serpents while keeping his eyes fixed firmly on the machine gun. The stench of smoke and stagnant water filled his nostrils as bullets whined past his ears and the ground threw up spurts of mud all around him, but then he was at the water's edge and he threw himself forward, diving for the gun.

As his fingers closed around the gun barrel he looked up and saw that he was less than a metre away from a huge, seething ball of the creatures. Almost as one they turned in his direction and began to slither across the grass towards him.

But Joe knew he wasn't going down without a

fight. Staggering to his feet, he pulled back the firing mechanism on the sub-machine gun, stared down the barrel and fired.

He took three of them apart before the first one reached him, still firing as it jumped up and smashed into his jaw, knocking him backwards and sending the gun flying from his hands. Crying out as sharp teeth tore at his body, he somehow managed to reach out and grab the barrel of the gun. He pulled it towards him, but just as his finger found the trigger, something struck him hard in the throat. The pain was excruciating, exploding into his head in a blur of blood and noise. Then suddenly, through all the confusion, he found himself staring up at a soft white moon and a sky full of stars.

Somewhere a long way off, he heard Harris shout, 'Keep firing! We've got them now! We've got them on the run!'

And as he rolled over onto his side he saw a black tide of the creatures, sated with blood, draw back and disappear into the canal.

All that remained was a stretch of grass, littered with wounded men and the bodies of serpents, glistening obscenely in the moonlight.

30

At first, he wasn't sure if he was dreaming, or even if he was still alive.

There was no screaming; no clatter of gunfire.

Only silence, washing the world clean.

His eyes flickered open. Was this heaven, this peaceful emptiness? If so, Joe decided, he liked it just fine. But as his eyelids grew heavy and began to close, he heard the squeak of a door opening, followed by the clunk and rattle of a trolley.

'Hello, my darlin'. How are you feeling?'

Joe opened his eyes to the sight of a smiling nurse in a white cap and blue uniform.

'You've had a nice long sleep. I expect you're ready for a spot of lunch aren't you?'

'Lunch?' Joe frowned. 'What time is it?'

'One o'clock,' said the nurse, helping him sit up. 'Lunchtime.'

As she plumped up his pillows, Joe noticed the

drip hanging above him, the tube in his arm and the screens around his bed.

'What am I doing here?' he asked.

'You've taken some nasty knocks,' said the nurse, 'but the doctors have been busy stitching you back together again.' She smiled. 'And I have to say, I think they've done a pretty good job.'

'Thanks,' said Joe, managing a weak smile in return. 'But what's wrong with me?'

'Well, let's put it this way, love,' replied the nurse as she wheeled a small table over his bed, 'you've got more stitches than a boxful of blankets and a nice set of bruises to go with them. But the good news is, there's no serious muscle damage.' She put a plate on the table in front of him and removed the cover, revealing a meal of sausage and beans. 'And if you manage to eat that lot up, I reckon we might have you back on your feet by teatime.'

Suddenly Joe's mind began to crowd with images: strange, fractured pictures of blood and smoke.

'Where are the others?' he asked.

'What others?'

'Giles, my dad – all the rest of them.'

The nurse frowned and shook her head.

'I don't know, sweetheart. We had so many in last night; we were rushed off our feet, to be honest. It was chaos. But I can try and find out for you. What did you say their names were?'

'My dad's called Martin McDonald. And my friend is called Giles. Giles Barclay.'

The nurse nodded and squeezed his hand. 'Martin McDonald and Giles Barclay,' she repeated. 'Alright, well you eat up your dinner and I'll see what I can find out for you, OK?'

'OK,' said Joe. As she steered the trolley towards the screens, Joe said quietly, 'Excuse me?'

The nurse stopped and looked at him.

'Yes, love?'

'The people who came in last night. Did any of them, you know . . .' his voice trailed off. 'Did any of them die?'

The nurse didn't reply right away.

'I don't know,' she said at last.

But Joe guessed that she did.

When she was gone, he pushed his plate of food away and lay back against the pillows, staring up at the ceiling. He dimly recalled lying in the back of an ambulance as the doors slammed shut. He remembered the *whup-whup-whup* of the siren and a young paramedic saying, *Shhh, you're alright, son*, before slipping a needle into the crook of his arm. But he didn't remember seeing Giles or his father.

He pressed his face into the palms of his hands, shutting out the light, and for the first time since the world had changed he began to cry. The tears dripped through his fingers and as he tasted the salt on his lips, it reminded him of the sea.

He was just drying his eyes when the door of the ward swung open. He heard the tap of footsteps across the tiled floor and then the face of the nurse appeared round the screen.

'Hello,' she said. 'I've brought someone to see you.'

She pulled back the screen and, as she stood back, Giles stepped through and gave him a little wave. He wore a blue hospital gown and clutched three limp irises in his fist.

'I brought these for you,' he said, smiling and holding them out in front of him. 'They actually belonged to a guy down the hall, but he's allergic, so . . .'

Joe looked at Giles, standing there in his hospital gown with wilting flowers and cuts on his face. And as he smiled and held up a fist as if they were champions of the world, he thought he had never been so glad to see anyone in his life.

The TV room was empty except for an old man sleeping in the corner. The nurse had been reluctant to let Joe out of the ward at first, but by the time Giles had finished telling her how the benefits of exercise would outweigh the risks she had practically levered him out of bed herself. And although he felt as though his body had been smashed to pieces and put together again in the wrong order, he was glad to be up.

The nurse had given him the good news that his dad was alive, but she had been unable to tell him much more, apart from the fact that he was safe. 'You needn't worry,' she said. 'He's in good hands.'

'So what happened?' Joe asked as Giles pulled up a couple of chairs and they settled down in front of the TV. 'Last thing I remember clearly is running to pick up that gun.'

Giles shook his head. 'That was *crazy*,' he said. 'When you shouted at me to cover you, everyone started blasting away, trying to keep those things away from you. But then they attacked and your dad waded in. And when we all started letting them have it, they just disappeared back into the canal. I got away with just a few bites on my leg, so I was pretty lucky.'

'Incredible,' said Joe. 'So what's the situation now?'

'See for yourself,' said Giles, switching on the TV. 'It's on all the channels.'

A reporter in a suit and tie stood at the end of a street cordoned off by a line of police tape. A red box appeared at the bottom of the screen with the words 'Breaking News' written across it. Behind the reporter were lines of police vans with their blue lights flashing. Soldiers were jumping out of trucks and being directed down the street by armed police officers.

'. . . and the same scene is being played out along every access point to the canal,' the reporter was saying. 'No one is allowed in or out. Houses in the area have been evacuated and local schools, churches and community halls are being used as temporary accommodation. Officials are saying it is merely a safety precaution but local people are understandably worried, particularly as at the moment, the nature of the threat remains unclear.'

'So what do you think?' asked Joe as the picture cut back to a newsreader in the studio, doing his best to look concerned on behalf of the nation. 'Do you think they can get rid of those things?'

'We'd better hope so,' said Giles, suddenly serious. 'Because like your dad said – if they can't, then those things are going to get rid of us.'

The sun went behind the clouds and a shadow swept across the room. Joe closed his eyes and imagined a dark tide of creatures swarming over streets and pavements, twisting and turning and hunting him down.

Opening his eyes once more, he looked at the old man sleeping in the corner and wondered if he would ever be able to sleep again.

31

Nodding at the armed policeman on the steps of the Home Office, Detective Sergeant Harris followed Superintendent Reeve through a maze of corridors and wondered what other surprises life had in store for him. What had begun as an apparently straight-forward murder case had spiralled into a deadly whirlwind whose path seemed impossible to predict.

No one had seen anything like it before and now they were having to make it up as they went along. People had died, questions were being asked and all the time the threat was still out there. Any minute now the media were going to get hold of the full story, and when they did, the public was going to need reassurance by the bucket load. But right now, reassurance was in short supply.

They were taken down some steps and along another corridor to a set of thick oak doors. Outside, two armed officers stood with sub-machine guns slung across their shoulders. As Reeve and Harris approached they pushed open the doors and waved them through.

Immediately, Harris recognised the Prime Minister sitting at the head of the table. To his left was the Home Secretary, and to his right the Metropolitan Police Commissioner. Most of the other seats were taken by various ministers and officials whom Harris did not recognise.

'Superintendent Reeve and Detective Sergeant Harris,' said the Metropolitan Police Commissioner, 'both from Avon & Somerset Police.'

'Welcome, gentlemen,' said the Prime Minister, turning to Superintendent Reeve. 'So tell us, Superintendent. What is the current situation?'

Reeve took a sip of water and set the glass down carefully on the table in front of him. 'The current situation,' he said, 'is that two members of the public and five police officers have died as a result of yesterday's attacks. Last night, however, armed officers located and destroyed fifteen of the creatures, the bodies of which have been taken to the London School of Hygiene and Tropical Medicine for analysis. Although many more creatures escaped back into the water, we have closed off the canal for three miles in either direction. Armed units are now patrolling the waterway, supported by detachments from the Royal Engineers and troops from the Air Assault Brigade. We are reasonably confident that, so far, the threat has been contained.'

'Reasonably confident?' The Prime Minister frowned. 'I'm not sure I like the sound of that. Perhaps you could expand on this, Superintendent?'

'Certainly, Prime Minister,' said Reeve. 'The Royal Engineers have installed concrete barriers six miles apart, effectively sealing off a whole section of the waterway, and have blocked all access to outflow pipes in that section. The next stage, already under-way, is to drain the canal. This will be done in sections using a lock-gate system. Once the water is removed, any remaining creatures will be exposed and destroyed.'

The Prime Minister nodded, taking it all in. 'Have we located the source of this invasion?'

'As far as we can gather,' Harris explained, 'a single specimen was brought back from an expedition to South America, but it seems that it is capable of reproducing by itself.'

'Hmm,' said a man in a dark suit, halfway down the table. 'Asexual reproduction. A way in which an individual organism can reproduce without the involvement of another member of the species. Are you absolutely sure about that?'

'This is Professor Wilson,' explained the Prime

Minister, 'from the London School of Hygiene and Tropical Medicine.'

'Oh,' said Harris, feeling out of his depth. 'Well, however it does it, it can certainly breed quicker than a shedload of rabbits.'

'Quite,' said the Prime Minister. 'In which case I think we must assume that these creatures will continue to multiply. How long will it take to drain the canal?'

'It should be completed by the end of the week,' said Reeve. 'After that it's simply a case of clearing the area and making it safe. If all goes to plan, we should have things back to normal inside a fortnight.'

'If all goes to plan,' echoed the Prime Minister. 'Now there's an interesting phrase, Superintendent Reeve, don't you think?'

To everyone's relief, the Prime Minister's worst fears appeared to be unfounded. The Royal Engineers worked with great efficiency, operating round the clock to drain a six-mile stretch of the canal. As each section was pumped out, heavily armed police and paratroopers trained their weapons on the water, waiting for the creatures to be revealed.

They were not disappointed. As water levels

dropped, the serpents came thrashing and squirming out of the mud, wriggling up the sides of the canal towards their tormentors. But this time the soldiers were ready for them. From carefully planned positions on lock gates and bridges, they waited until the serpents were clear of the mud before opening fire with automatic rifles, heavy machine guns and 30mm cannon. The resulting firepower was so intense that the serpents were cut to ribbons long before they even made it to land, pounded back into the mud by a hail of bullets. The whole of the city's drainage system was flushed through with a powerful disinfectant solution that no living organism could survive contact with.

At a meeting of COBRA, the government's emergency committee, US security officials reported that they had been in contact with Dave Moreton's team in Mexico and everything had been reported as normal. There had been no further sightings of the mysterious creatures and it was generally agreed that it would be irresponsible to cause further panic until the facts were established beyond reasonable doubt.

So the newspapers were fed a story about the creatures being brought back from a different rainforest expedition that Sims had been on the previous year. After all, everyone knew that rainforests were full of all kinds of weird stuff that no one had ever heard of. And besides, the rainforest in question was in the middle of a country which was busy ploughing it up at a rate of over an acre per second, which meant they wouldn't be too bothered about the adverse publicity.

The media lapped it up, of course, pointing the finger at irresponsible scientists and calling for greater controls on the import of animals from other countries. All across the country, people held their loved ones a little closer as they began to imagine the possibilities of new and unknown dangers. There were questions asked about human interference and angry exchanges in Parliament during Prime Minister's Question Time, accusing the government of playing with people's lives. But when the Prime Minister said sternly, 'We were not playing with lives, we were *saving* them,' it was widely quoted and people began to feel reassured: there had been a crisis, the authorities had acted quickly, and now the crisis was over.

Or at least, that was what everyone thought.

32

Five thousand miles away on the other side of the world, Professor Dave Moreton sat in the passenger seat of a hired jeep as it bounced along the rough dirt track, clouds of orange dust trailing in its wake. Alongside the track were piles of logs, drying and cracking in the hot sun. Beyond the log piles were dead stumps, marking the place where once there had been a rainforest, teeming with life.

But now the rich, moist earth had turned to dust. Nothing grew here any more. Moreton stared at the distant rainforest and wondered how long it would be before that was gone too.

It had been strange leaving the team and flying back to Washington. He'd been summoned at short notice to meet with some government people and they'd seemed rather on edge, asking him all kinds of questions about the things he'd seen when the sub first went down. But when he'd reassured them that everything was fine and there had been no sightings since, they'd all seemed to relax. Come to think of it, one of them might even have smiled. But it hadn't stopped them from sending a team down.

So here he was, driving into the Mexican jungle with a bunch of guys in sweats and Ray-Bans who wouldn't have looked out of place in a Bond movie. That was the thing about this job. You never knew what to expect from one day to the next.

Linder, the guy driving the jeep, turned to look at him and Moreton saw the road reflected in his shades.

'Where is everyone? Or don't these guys show up for work until after lunch?'

'Who knows?' Moreton looked out at the trucks and tractors, the winch cranes and the pick-ups, and realised that the place was empty of people. It was kind of strange. Any time he'd been past before, the place had always been alive with lumber managers shouting over the buzz of chainsaws, trying to get the most out of their temporary workers. 'Maybe it's some kind of holiday.'

'Maybe.' Linder wiped the sweat from his forehead. 'How much further 'til we get to your place?'

'Not far. Once we get into the forest it's only a couple of miles or so.'

Twenty minutes later they drove into the damp,

shadowy heat of the rainforest. As the trees closed around them, Linder lifted his foot from the accelerator and the jeep slowed to a crawl.

It's good to be back, thought Moreton.

Tipping his head back, he looked up at the thick lattice of branches, countless shades of green punctuated by the occasional splinter of blue sky.

'Hey,' said Linder, interrupting his thoughts. 'What's that?'

Moreton frowned. 'What's what?'

Linder brought the car to a halt and pointed into the trees.

'That. Up there.'

Moreton followed Linder's gaze to where the thick stems of a strangler fig wrapped themselves around a ceiba tree, scrambling up toward the light. Fifteen metres above the ground, where thick vines hung festooned from the branches, Moreton saw the body of a man. He was dressed in blue jeans and a white shirt. Except that the white shirt was no longer white. And it had been torn to pieces, just like the unfortunate man who was wearing it.

'Look!' shouted Mason from the back seat. 'Over there!'

Moreton spun round and saw that Mason was pointing up into the trees behind them. At first, his mind refused to believe what his eyes were telling him. But as he continued to stare, Moreton realised that he had not been mistaken. The trees were full of bodies. Ten, twenty, maybe even thirty of them, hanging up in the trees as if they had simply fallen from the sky.

'Oh no,' whispered Moreton. 'Oh please, no.'

Linder turned to Moreton, hoping for some kind of answer. 'What do you think?' he asked in a hushed voice. 'A plane crash, maybe?'

But the answer, when it came, was from a quite different direction.

Moreton heard the buzz of wings a second before Linder screamed. Then something knocked him sideways out of the jeep and his head hit the thick roots of a papaya tree. Pain exploded behind his eyes and for a moment the world dissolved in a whirl of light and colour. He breathed the scent of damp earth and heard the gentle ticking of the jeep's engine. He rolled over onto his back, brushing dirt and leaves from his face. For a moment he was confused, unsure of what was real and what was imagined. But as he looked up and saw the bodies cradled in the trees, the truth hit him and he struggled to his knees.

'Linder! Mason!' he called. 'You OK?'

But there was only silence. And as he stumbled towards the jeep, he saw that the seats were empty.

The others were nowhere to be seen.

Reaching into the cab, Moreton turned off the ignition and the engine died.

'Hey, guys!' he shouted into the stillness of the forest. 'Where are you?'

High in the trees, something moved. Moreton looked up and saw the grey shadows plummeting towards him. Then he began to run, whimpering like a frightened animal who knows that the hunters are coming.

33

Joe sat at the kitchen table, eating a bowl of cereal and watching a sparrow peck at some stale bread on the lawn. After leaving hospital he became something of a local hero for a while, the papers calling him and Giles 'The Dragonslayers' and recommending them both for bravery awards. It was all very nice, what with all the attention and everything, but after a week or so the papers moved on to stories about plane crashes, celebrity diets and house prices, and life gradually returned to normal.

Yesterday he'd had his stitches out and now the pain was almost gone; for the first time, he had slept through the night.

'You know what I was thinking?' asked his dad, ambling into the room and switching on the kettle. 'I was thinking we both *really* need a holiday.'

Joe looked at his dad, leaning against the kitchen counter in his T-shirt and jeans, and thought how different he seemed. Before the attack he had always been out of the house by eight in the morning, too busy for holidays, too busy for weekends, too busy for conversation even. But now . . .

'Are you serious?'

'Absolutely. What do you say?'

Joe smiled.

'That'd be great,' he said.

Walking in the shade of the limes that grew along the pavement, Joe passed the bright red post box, the empty bus shelter, the newsagent's and the charity shop, and as the light reflected from windows and shone off the bumpers and bonnets of parked cars, he realised that the greyness inside him was burning away at last.

His dad was going into the university this morning to tie up a few loose ends. Then, for the first time in years, he was going to take a couple of weeks off. On Saturday they would throw their stuff into the van and drive down to the coast. Joe could almost taste the salt on his lips and feel the sand between his toes.

What was it they said about every cloud having a silver lining?

It had been one heck of a cloud, but the edges were getting shinier by the minute.

* * *

'Thought I might find you here,' said Joe, shielding his eyes against the sun. He peered up at the tree-house and saw that Giles was reading. As Joe appeared at the top of the ladder he closed his book and offered Joe his hand.

'Mr McDonald,' he said. 'Or should I call you "Dragonslayer"?'

'You can if you like,' said Joe, grabbing Giles's hand and pulling himself up. 'But I think I prefer Joe.'

Giles led the way into the treehouse. As Joe made himself comfortable on the cushions, he unscrewed his flask and poured out two cups of ice-cold lemonade.

'How's your mum?' Joe asked. 'Any better?'

Giles nodded and handed him a cup. 'She's coming home tomorrow.'

'That's great.' Joe paused. 'You know, you could have stayed with us while she was in hospital. My dad was absolutely fine with it. I told you that, didn't I?'

'Yeah, thanks. That's where I told Social Services I was. But to be honest, I'm happy looking after myself. I'm used to it, remember?' He paused and took a sip of lemonade. 'You know, your dad's a good man, Joe. Mum told me that when he was in hospital, he came to visit her every day. To make sure she was alright.'

'My dad? Really?'

'Yeah. I know she really appreciated it.'

Joe looked through the doorway and watched the sun stream through the leaves in a blaze of green.

'I still can't believe any of this,' he said.

Giles nodded 'Makes you think, though, doesn't it. But then, "Everything is sweetened by risk". I read that when I came out of hospital. It made me think about all this stuff we've been going through. I mean, it's been terrible and everything. But now it's done and we're still alive, I'm thinking, would I have wanted to miss it? And the answer is, probably not. Don't get me wrong, I'm not saying I would have chosen it. But still . . .'

'I know what you mean,' said Joe. 'Somehow it feels as if we weren't really living before. And now that it's over, it feels . . . different.'

'Different worse or different better?'

'Different better, I think. But I'm glad it's over.'

Joe was about to take another sip of lemonade, when he heard a curious sound, a *brrrrrrrp!* like someone flipping through a deck of cards.

'What was that?' he asked, turning to look at Giles.

'I don't know,' said Giles. 'But I'm not sure I like the sound of it.'

34

'There it is again,' said Giles.

The noise was fainter this time, more distant.

They climbed out through the doorway and Joe balanced himself against the tree trunk, peering through a curtain of leaves.

'Can you see anything?' he asked.

'No,' said Giles. 'But I think it came from somewhere above us.'

Joe tilted his head back and caught sight of something at the top of the tree.

'Hey,' he said. 'Come and look at this.'

Giles stepped back across the branch and Joe pointed up at the strange object. It was partially hidden by leaves, but appeared to be a long cylindrical shape.

'Let's take a closer look,' said Giles.

Two minutes later they were ten metres above the ground, balancing on a thin branch and staring at a large, papery tube about the size of a sleeping bag. There were regular bumps and ridges along its length and it was attached to the trunk with a white, sticky thread. The top half was ripped open, as though something had torn its way out.

'Now that,' whispered Giles. 'is *weird.*'

Joe remembered something then.

Walking through the fields one summer, his father teaching him the names of wild flowers: cowslip, heartsease, coltsfoot and pennywort. They had come to a river and walked alongside it for a while, looking at small fish swimming over polished stones. After reaching a bend in the river there had been a clump of bulrushes, straight and tall, growing up out of the water. And it was here, on the stem of one of the bulrushes, that Joe had seen something very like what he was seeing now.

Except this one was a hundred times bigger.

'Giles, we have to move,' he said. 'We have to get out of here now.'

'Why?' Giles saw the fear in Joe's eyes and realised that something was wrong. 'What's the matter?'

'Look,' said Joe, pointing to a faint, silver trail on the side of the tree. 'Recognise that?'

Giles stared in disbelief. 'But surely they killed them all, didn't they?'

Joe tapped the edge of the papery tube and they

listened to the hollow echo inside. 'I don't think so. You know what this is, don't you?'

'What?'

'It's like the things dragonfly larvae leave on plant stems when they turn into adult dragonflies.'

Giles looked worried.

'You think that's what this is? Some kind of giant chrysalis?'

'I don't know. But maybe those serpents were just the first stage in the life cycle of something else. And maybe some of them managed to get out of the canal before it was drained.'

'If so,' said Giles, 'then where have they gone?'

Before Joe could reply, there was a loud buzzing sound and several leaves fluttered down from the top of a nearby tree.

'Look,' Giles whispered. 'Over there.'

Clinging to the tree trunk was a huge insect. Its grey, smoke-coloured wings were folded across its back and six rough-bristled legs held fast to the bark, each one as long as Joe's arm.

The creature had emerged from the chrysalis transformed. Where once it had been supple and snake-like, now it was covered in a hard brown exoskeleton from which uniform bumps and ridges rose like tiny mountain ranges, protecting it from attack like a suit of armour. Protruding from the top of its head was a pair of blood-red eyes, bulging like angry boils as they swivelled to and fro, scanning the trees for signs of movement. As Joe gasped in horror and pressed back against the tree, the insect crawled further up the trunk, its wings vibrating loudly. Suddenly, all around them, the treetops began to buzz and vibrate. And as Joe looked up he noticed that most of the trees had empty cases attached to their trunks.

'What do we do now?' he whispered. 'If we move they'll see us.'

High in the treetops, the buzzing grew louder as the creatures flew from their resting places and began to gather amongst the leaves.

'If we stay here we're dead,' said Giles, pressing his face against the tree trunk. 'It's only a matter of time before they see us.'

Every instinct screamed at Joe to get away as fast as possible. But he knew that moving too quickly would be suicide. If the insects spotted them, they wouldn't get beyond the path before they were ripped apart.

'Giles,' he whispered. 'Is the house open?'

'Yeah. Why?'

'Because if we can get inside, at least we'll have a chance. But we'll have to make it through the trees without being seen.'

Joe held on to the branch with his left hand and leaned back, trying to see where the creatures had gathered.

'There's a group of them in that tree over there,' he said, watching two more fly through the branches and settle amongst the others. 'Have a look on your side, see if you can see any more.'

Giles inched his way around the tree. He held the branch above him for support and stepped back to look.

'Careful,' Joe warned. 'Don't let them see you.'

Giles pulled himself back and sucked air through his teeth.

'Three of them. Two on the tree to the left and another in the middle.'

Joe thought for a second. 'I reckon we've got a clear line through the trees on the right. But we need to take it slow. If they see any signs of move-ment, they're going to come looking.'

Giles leaned back to check one last time, then nodded.

'Ready?'

'Ready as I'll ever be.'

'Alright. Let's go.'

For a second or two Joe was unable to move, aware that the creatures might already be watching him. But he pushed the thought from his mind and began his slow, careful descent. As the buzzing grew louder, he tried not to think about the moment when the flies would see them. About the moment when they would swivel their blood-red eyes and descend from the trees like a plague from hell.

35

Kenneth Wilkinson was a watch-mender by trade, and it was a job that he had always found most gratifying. He liked the order and neatness of it; the way all the cogs and gears fitted together just so, with nothing out of place and everything as it should be. There was something deeply satisfying about putting the last piece in place and listening to the regular tick-tick-tick of everything working together, each small part moving in sweet, harmonious perfection.

In contrast, however, Kenneth had always viewed the world as something of a disappointment. In many ways it was like one big timepiece, the movements of sun and moon marking out the passage of time: the days, weeks, summers and winters.

This was most acceptable.

But what annoyed him were the people who swarmed all over it. They reminded him of dust particles, clogging up the mechanism. Already their interference with the workings meant it got harder each year to tell the difference between the seasons. There was no doubt about it; the world would run more smoothly without them. But people weren't like dust, of course; one couldn't just wipe the mechanism clean. What they needed was guidance. Somebody to show them how to make things work.

Which was why, for the past fourteen years, Kenneth Wilkinson had been Chair of the Parish Council.

Bringing order to the whole world might be somewhat beyond his reach, but bringing it to his local parish was most definitely not. And with all the strange goings-on recently, the local parish needed all the help it could get.

'I don't wish to be rude, Mr Wilkinson,' said Diana Bennett – a sure sign, thought Kenneth, that she was about to be – 'but is this going to take much longer?'

'I'm sorry, Diana,' Kenneth replied, peering at her over the top of his half-moon spectacles. 'Is there somewhere else you have to be?'

'It's not me,' said Diana, 'it's my dogs. They're in the Range Rover, and although I've left the windows open, it's a very hot day out there. I'd hate for them to be uncomfortable.'

Kenneth didn't like dogs. And he particularly didn't like Diana Bennett's dogs, because – as far as he could tell – they didn't like him either. They were big Alsatians and whenever he passed them they would bare their teeth in a most disagreeable manner. But he didn't want anything to spoil his big moment, so he smiled thinly and said, 'Just another ten minutes or so, Diana, and then we'll be finished. Do you think they can possibly hold out until then?'

Diana's face took on a look of pained resignation. 'I suppose so, yes.'

'Jolly good. Moving on, then . . .'

Kenneth took a cream-coloured letter from his pocket, placed it face down on the table and turned to the last item on the agenda.

'Item seven,' he said, neatly circling the number with his gold-tipped fountain pen, 'is the repair of the canal. As you know, the local authority has been dragging its heels over this, so I took it upon myself to write to the Prime Minister.'

As he paused to allow his words time to sink in, he was gratified to see the looks of surprise around the table.

'The Prime Minister?' whispered Margaret who ran the flower shop on the corner of Station Road. 'You wrote to the Prime Minister?'

'Yes,' replied Kenneth, trying unsuccessfully not

to sound too pleased with himself. 'And what's more, the Prime Minister wrote back.' Carefully unfolding the letter so that everyone might see its golden crest, Kenneth cleared his throat and began to read.

Dear Mr Wilkinson,

Thank you for your letter, which I received today. I was sorry to learn that the canal has been left in a poor state. You will understand, of course, that the emergency measures carried out in previous weeks were essential to main- tain public health and safety. However, given the unusual circumstances, I am instructing the Treasury to make funds immediately available so that the canal may be restored to its former glory. I hope this meets with your approval and I look forward to receiving the news that work has been completed in the very near future.

Kenneth looked up, paused for dramatic effect and then added: '*Yours sincerely* . . . and look,' – here he held up the letter for the others to see – 'it's signed by the Prime Minister himself.'

'Oh, Ken,' said Margaret, her face bright with admiration. 'That's absolutely marvellous.'

'It wouldn't have anything to do with the local elec- tion coming up next month, I suppose?' said Gareth Harper, who still hadn't forgiven the government for putting up his council tax.

'I don't care what it's got to do with,' said Margaret, who had been doodling flower patterns in the margin of her notebook. 'I think it's wonderful news, and I think we should all propose a vote of thanks to Kenneth for once again showing us what can be achieved through hard work and persistence.'

'Hear, hear,' said everyone except Gareth Harper. But even he nodded in surly agreement, and although Kenneth held up his hands and said, 'No, please, I have only done what anyone would have done in the circumstances,' he knew that this was not true, and that he had done a very good thing. And of this he was quietly proud.

As he locked the door of the village hall and followed the others down the grassy path towards the road, Kenneth felt the same way he did whenever he took out a broken watch spring and replaced it with a new one. It was a feeling that – in his own small way – he had restored some order to the world and made it better than before.

The feeling, however, was short lived.

As Bill Higgins stopped on the path and waited for him to catch up, Kenneth became aware of a strange sound, like the hum from a power station. It seemed to be coming from the line of beech trees that marked the border between the footpath and the field.

'Do you hear that?' Bill asked.

Kenneth nodded. 'Yes, I hear it.'

The others had stopped further up the path, listening.

Suddenly the gardener from the village hall appeared at the top of the path and began running towards them, his spade clutched tightly in his hand.

'Run!' he shrieked, his voice shaky and fretful like that of a frightened child. 'RUN!'

'What is it, John?' asked Kenneth. 'Whatever's the matter?'

But the gardener just kept running and Kenneth had to step back in order to avoid a collision.

This was all very confusing. The world he had restored to order only minutes before now appeared to be fraying at the edges, allowing strange noises and mad gardeners to come creeping through at the seams.

There had to be a reason for it, of course.

A simple, logical explanation.

And as Kenneth looked up into the air he saw what it was: a dark, buzzing cloud that lifted from the trees and fell out of the sky towards him.

Before Kenneth knew what was happening, something thumped into his shoulder and knocked him to the ground. Raising his arms to protect his face, he heard screams from further down the path and felt a sharp, searing pain across his arm. He realised that whatever had knocked him down was now tearing at his flesh and if it didn't stop soon, he was going to die an extremely painful death.

Struggling to break free, Kenneth whimpered as he saw the red, insect-like eyes staring down at him. This was not the peaceful world order he had hoped for.

This was the world trying to kill him.

The creature opened its mouth and razor-sharp jaws slashed agonisingly across his forehead. Something crunched down on his legs and there was a scrabbling, biting mess as the pain increased and all he could do was scream and claw at the hideous nightmare that flapped and buzzed above him.

Then Kenneth heard a growl, followed by a thump. He felt hot breath in his ear and thought: *This is it. This is where I die . . .*

But Kenneth did not die.

Instead, the blackness lifted and through a film of blood he saw what appeared to be a large insect with smoke-coloured wings being dragged across the path. As he staggered to his feet he saw that its

208

attacker was a large Alsatian. Snapping and snarling, the powerful animal ripped the creature's wings off before leaping on it once more, shaking it from side to side until it stopped moving altogether. Kenneth heard more buzzing and then, with a low growl, a second dog launched itself into the air. It caught one of the insects in mid-flight and brought it crashing to the ground where both dogs immediately set upon it in a frenzy of barking and yelping.

Seeing his chance, Kenneth ran away down the path towards Bill Higgins, who was calling for help from beneath another of the creatures. For the first time, Kenneth saw the sheer size of the insect. Its wingspan was wider than his outstretched arms and as it thrashed and buzzed around on the path, he began to wonder if the world was coming to an end. But Kenneth knew this was not the time for such fanciful thoughts. Employing the same technique he had used on the rugby fields of his youth, he ran forward and kicked the huge insect with all his remaining strength. It flew sideways, hit one of the fence posts and became entangled in the barbed wire. Kenneth watched as it struggled furiously, twisting its body and flapping its wings in an effort to break free.

'Come on!' he yelled, pulling Higgins to his feet. 'Let's go!'

The two men sprinted to the end of the path where they discovered Diana Bennett waiting for them. The doors of her Range Rover were already open and Margaret was sitting in the front seat, sobbing hysterically. Gareth was huddled in the back seat behind her.

'Come on, you two!' Diana urged as they stumbled across the pavement, bright droplets of blood splashing onto the kerb. 'Get a move on!'

Kenneth pushed the terrified Higgins into the back of the Range Rover and threw himself after him. Diana Bennett stood on the pavement with her arms folded like a scoutmistress awaiting the return of her troop.

'Diana!' he yelled as the creatures began to swarm above them, darkening the sky. 'Get inside!'

'In a minute,' she said. 'I'm just waiting for my boys.' Kenneth saw that three of the creatures were now circling directly over her head.

'Diana!' he shouted. 'You have to come now!'

Diana ignored him and walked to the end of the path, cupping her hands around her mouth and shouting, 'Tiger! Carson! Come here!'

Seconds later the two dogs came yelping and barking out onto the pavement, their fur streaked with blood and dirt.

'In you go, chaps!' Diana instructed them. The

two dogs leapt up onto the back seat, knocking Kenneth sideways into Bill Higgins's lap. As Diana slammed the door, Kenneth looked through the side window and saw one of the huge flies streaking out of the sky towards her. Banging frantically on the window, he watched in horror as it folded its wings and plummeted towards the back of her head.

'Diana!' he screamed. 'Watch out!'

Diana looked up, saw the insect approaching and calmly lifted her walking stick. The fly tried to change course at the last second, but it was too late. With a *thwalpp!* it crunched into the metal tip and impaled itself upon the stick like some awful, writhing kebab. The force of the impact knocked Diana to the pavement but she simply got to her feet again, dusted herself down and climbed into the driver's seat.

'Wretched thing,' she said. 'Ruined a perfectly good walking stick.' Then she turned the key in the ignition and accelerated away from the kerb as another of the creatures slammed into the windscreen. 'Good grief,' she said, turning on the wipers and watching it slide off into the road. 'Persistent little blighters, aren't they?'

In the back seat Kenneth sat open mouthed as Diana increased her speed and more giant insects thudded against the roof and windows. Then he leaned back and closed his eyes. As one of the Alsatians began to lick his face, Kenneth put a grateful arm around its neck. In this strange, uncertain world, one thing was for sure.

Dogs were now officially Kenneth Wilkinson's favourite animals.

36

'Whatever you do, don't move,' said Giles. 'I can see one on your right.'

Joe froze. 'Are you sure?' he whispered, gingerly turning his head. 'I can't see anything.' It had taken five agonising minutes to climb down the rope ladder and now, as he waited nervously on the bottom rung, he could feel his heart thumping in his chest.

'Over there,' said Giles. 'Hidden in the ivy.'

As Joe stared at the cluster of shiny leaves wrapped around a nearby sycamore tree, he noticed a pair of red eyes, gleaming dully in the shadows. 'OK,' he said, his fingers tightening around the rope ladder. 'I see it now.'

He waited, motionless, terrified that the creature might have seen him. After a minute or so he whispered, 'Giles, we can't stay here all day.'

'We might have to,' said Giles.

'Not necessarily. Look at the angle of it. If we

move back behind that tree, we'll be out of its line of sight.'

'Are you sure?'

'No.'

There was a long pause.

'Alright,' said Giles at last. 'But let's take it *real* slow, OK?'

Gripping the rope ladder, Joe lowered his feet to the ground, making sure there were no twigs to snap and give away their position.

'Go down,' hissed Giles.

'I *am* down,' said Joe.

'No, go *down*,' Giles repeated, moving his hand up and down as if he was bouncing an invisible basketball. 'It'll make you harder to see.'

Joe bent his knees and slid forward onto his stomach. He listened, trying to pick out any possible sounds of movement. But all he could hear was the buzzing in the trees and the faint creak of the rope ladder as Giles made his way down.

'OK,' said Giles, sliding next to him. 'So far so good.'

Joe put his weight on his forearms and began crawling towards the next tree, stopping every few seconds to peer up through the branches. He could see the spindly legs poking out through the ivy, but he knew it wasn't far to the edge of the woods now.

If they really went for it, they could probably make it from there to the house in less than ten seconds.

'Keep going!' urged Giles. 'We're almost there.'

Joe wriggled forward like a snake in the dust. Then he got cautiously to his feet and stood behind the tree, pressing his arms against his sides to make himself as inconspicuous as possible.

Giles stood next to him and looked around.

'They're behind us now,' said Joe. 'We should be able to make it inside before they can get to us.'

'You think?'

Joe wiped sweat from his eyes.

'There's only one way to find out.'

Now that the moment had arrived, his stomach fluttered as if he was standing on the edge of a high cliff. The world seemed so precious – the smell of the earth, the warm sun and the green leaves – he could hardly bear the thought that it might soon be gone.

But there was no turning back, and they both knew it.

'Alright,' he said, clenching his fists. 'Ready?'

'Ready,' said Giles.

Joe took one last look behind him.

'After three,' he said. 'One, two . . . three!'

As they broke cover, Joe took off after Giles and felt the air blur around him, his feet thudding across the dry ground as his legs pumped faster and faster. The house was getting nearer now, nearer with every second and relief began to push through his fear because surely now the distance was too great and the creatures were too far back to reach them. But then suddenly Giles screamed 'Stop!' and held out his arm, and as Joe skidded to a halt he saw that one of the insects had flown down from the roof and landed on the patio in front of them.

There was no time to think. As Giles grabbed a brick from the pile at the edge of the patio, Joe spotted Giles's cricket bat propped up against the wall. He snatched it up at the same moment that Giles threw the brick and they both watched it skim the creature's head before shattering against the wall behind it. With an angry buzz, the fly swivelled round to face them.

'Giles!' Joe yelled as Giles grabbed another brick. 'Throw it at me!'

At first Giles didn't understand. But as Joe raised the bat and the fly lifted up into the air, realisation dawned on him and he pitched a looping throw just in front of Joe's face.

Joe saw the dark blur of the insect at the edge of his vision and knew it was flying towards him. But his focus was on the brick and for a fraction of a second the world seemed to slow down, just long enough for his brain to calculate its exact position in time and space. Then the bat cracked against it and the brick flew off like a bullet, striking the insect in mid-flight and spinning it against the wall, where it fell to the ground in a tattered heap.

'Oh, *sweet!*' cried Giles.

But it was no time for celebration. Sensing the vibrations, two more of the creatures fluttered down from the roof and began flying across the grass towards them.

'Throw!' shouted Joe. 'THROW!'

As Giles threw another brick, Joe swung the bat and missed. 'Dammit!' he shouted. 'Pitch it higher!'

This time Giles flipped the brick in a slow, looping arc and, as it dropped in front of him, Joe swung the bat so hard that stone chips flew off and struck him in the face. But he didn't take his eyes off the brick until it slammed into the approaching fly and took it apart in mid-air, fragments of legs and wings fluttering down like ash from a bonfire.

But then the second insect slammed Giles sideways into the pile of bricks, scattering them in all directions. As Giles cried out in pain, Joe ran forward and swung the bat hard into the creature's mid-section. Squelching like a squashed yoghurt carton, the fly crumpled and shot off into the trees, smacking against a branch before falling down into the bushes. Joe heard a low hum from the treetops and looked up to see a huge swarm lifting into the air, spreading across the sky like thunderclouds.

'Go!' shouted Joe, dropping the bat. 'Go, go, go!'

Grabbing Giles's arm, he pulled him to his feet and they ran across the patio towards the French windows. Joe pushed down on the handle, but it wouldn't budge. He tried again, rattling it frantically, but still it wouldn't move.

'It's locked, Giles!' he shouted. 'You must have bolted it before you came out!'

Giles stared back at him with wide, unfocussed eyes and Joe realised that he was suffering from shock. Over his shoulder he could see huge swarms of insects descending from the trees. In desperation, he looked around and saw two paving stones propped up against the wall. Gritting his teeth, he lifted one up onto his knees and flung it at the window. But the stone was too heavy and it slipped from his grasp, shattering into pieces on the patio. Shouting with frustration, he grabbed Giles by the shoulders and shook him.

'Giles, you *have* to help me! Help me lift the other stone!'

Giles blinked and, as the shadows of the insects swept towards them across the lawn, Joe saw the fear return to his eyes. Together they lifted the stone and ran at the window, glass shattering around them as they smashed their way through into the living room.

'The swords!' Joe shouted as shards of glass rained down onto the carpet. He pulled one off the wall and threw it to Giles before grabbing the other one for himself.

The sky was alive now. Joe turned to see five huge flies swooping fast and low across the garden. He saw the blurred wings and the twitch of jaws as they approached, their eyes the colour of dried blood.

'Here they come!' shouted Giles.

Joe gripped the sword in both hands, knowing he was probably going to die.

'Alright,' he said, surprised at how calm his voice sounded. 'They can't all get through at once. They've got to come through the hole in the glass. And when they do, we let them have it, OK?'

White-faced, Giles raised his sword and nodded.

'OK. Let's do it.'

Joe's fingers tightened around the sword's handle and a trickle of sweat ran down his back. Seconds later the flies thumped against the window, their wiry legs scrabbling at the glass as they searched for a way in. Joe saw one of them fix its eyes on him, its head swivelling, first one way then another, as if trying to work out how to get to him. It spotted the hole in the window, flew back a short distance and with a loud buzzing of wings, smashed its way through the glass.

As Joe recoiled in horror, Giles thrust his sword forward with such force that the blade went clean through the insect's body. But the power of its wings kept it flying, driving Giles backward as it continued to buzz and snap at his face. Stumbling against the far wall, Giles regained his balance and swung the sword sideways, flinging the creature across the room where it smashed into the Welsh dresser. As glass and crockery crashed to the floor, Joe turned to see another of the insects wriggling through the broken window. Spinning on his heel, he brought the sword up so hard and fast that the blade sliced the creature's head off, sending it bouncing across the carpet. The headless body thumped heavily to the floor and skidded against the sofa in a bloody tumble of wings. Beyond it, Joe saw more dark shapes dropping out of the sky and knew that the swarm was heading straight for them. As a third fly crashed through the window Giles and Joe both thrust their swords forward at the same time, pinning the buzzing creature against the sofa like some hideous museum exhibit.

They were all over the window now; it would only be a matter of time before they found their way through.

'Come on!' shouted Giles, thumping Joe on the arm. 'Let's go!'

As two more of them flew into the room, Joe followed Giles into the hallway and slammed the door behind him. But the kitchen window had been left open and insects were already pouring through it.

'Upstairs!' Joe cried. As he pounded up the staircase, several flies flew up at the banisters but Joe punched them away with his fist like a quarterback running for the line. His lungs bursting, he leapt up onto the landing and ran towards Giles's bedroom, falling through the doorway a fraction of a second before Giles landed on top of him. Pushing him off, Joe sprang to his feet and kicked the door shut. As he caught his breath, he noticed that the bedroom was growing darker and turned to see a cloud of insects swarming outside the window. They began to land on the glass and with each new thump, the bedroom grew darker still.

Giles turned on the television and they watched in silence as a news flash showed roads jammed with abandoned cars and pavements littered with bodies and broken glass. Swarms of flies were spreading out across the city and people were screaming, running for cover as they swept down from the sky. A frightened reporter crouched behind some dustbins while a shaky cameraman panned round to show the insects landing in streets and gardens all around them. Then, as the reporter dropped his microphone and began to run, the camera tipped sideways and the picture disappeared in a snowstorm of static.

Giles swore and turned off the TV.

'Listen,' he whispered. 'Do you hear that?'

At first all Joe could hear was a faint scratching. But soon it became louder, more intense, like a thousand fingernails scraping down a blackboard.

'You know what they're doing, don't you?' said Giles quietly.

Joe shook his head. 'What?'

'Look,' said Giles, pointing at the glass. 'They're chewing through the frame.'

And as Joe watched the insects tearing at the wood with their powerful jaws, he heard a scratching sound outside the bedroom door and realised that Giles was right.

They would be through in minutes.

And this time there was nowhere to run.

37

Professor Moreton stumbled out of the forest into the blinding sun. To his left was the tent which housed all the expedition's computer equipment. Beside it were three 4x4s and the mobile crane with the orange sub still dangling from its winch. A hundred metres in front of him were the dark waters of El Zacatón. The fact that this place had been his life for the past few weeks meant nothing to him now.

This was partly because everyone else on the programme was dead, lying in the forest like lumps of discarded meat.

But it was also because he was dying. Gazing down at his blood-soaked shirt, he felt the life draining out of him. The dream of success he had hoped to find in the depths of El Zacatón had turned into a nightmare, crawling from its dark waters to wreak havoc in the world.

But even now, in these final moments, the biologist

in Moreton saw that this was simply the world trying to restore the balance. Like a patient caught in the grip of a fever, it was trying to rid itself of the human organisms that threatened to overwhelm it. The huge insects had become growth-limiting factors for the human race.

But now, it seemed, the insects were encountering some growth-limiting factors of their own.

And it was this final observation which offered him a faint glimmer of hope.

Not for him, of course.

It was too late for that.

But as he fell to his knees and looked at the hundreds of creatures strewn across the clearing, flapping and dying like fish on a beach, he remembered the boy on the other side of the world and knew there was one last thing he had to do.

Reaching into his pocket, he pulled out his phone.

38

The buzzing was deafening now. Joe and Giles had tried pushing the bed and the wardrobe against the window, but they couldn't create a proper barrier. Joe had been frightened many times over the past few weeks, but as he stared into the eyes of the creatures whose only ambition was to tear him apart, he knew that this was far worse than anything he had seen before.

This time they were trapped with no chance of escape.

So this is it, he thought. *In spite of everything, the world will get me in the end . . .*

But then, beneath the buzzing of wings, he heard a different noise.

A vibration.

He looked round and saw Giles grab his phone from the shelf.

'Yes?' Giles was staring straight ahead, unable to

take his eyes off the insects as they chewed through the window frame. 'OK, one second.' He handed the phone to Joe.

'It's for you.'

'Hello?' Joe pressed the phone to his ear and heard, very faintly, a man's voice on the other end of the line.

'You were right,' it whispered. 'I should have believed you. I'm sorry.'

'Professor Moreton?' he asked shakily. 'Professor Moreton, is that you?'

'Joe, listen, you have to warn everyone. Tell them they're dealing with killing machines. And then, whatever you do, just get yourself out of there. You don't want to be around when those things hatch out.'

Joe looked at the monstrous flies crawling across the glass. He watched their jaws tearing at the window frame and listened to the wood splinter.

'It's too late for that,' he said. 'They're already here.'

'Jee elleffus,' croaked Moreton. 'Jee elleffus wasps . . .'

'Hello?' Joe shouted into the phone. 'Professor Moreton? Are you there?'

But the line was dead and Joe threw the phone back on the shelf.

'What did he say?' asked Giles, desperately wedging a chair under the door handle as the scratching on the other side became more frantic.

'Something about jee elleffus wasps.' The buzzing grew louder and Joe found himself having to shout above the noise. 'Mean anything to you?'

'No.' Giles stared white-faced at the insects scrabbling at the glass. 'I don't get it. They don't look anything like wasps.'

Joe put his hands over his ears and tried to concentrate.

Jee elleffus wasps, jee elleffus wasps.

Whatever did Moreton mean?

'Wait,' he said, suddenly clicking his fingers and pointing at Giles. 'I don't think he was talking about the flies. I think he was saying the letters.'

Giles stared at him.

'What letters?'

'The letters *G, L, F*. I think he was saying that the GLF is wasps.'

Giles looked nervously at the window.

'Joe, you're not making any sense.'

'GLF. Growth-limiting factor, remember? My dad talked about it. It's the thing that stops any one organism from spreading and taking over.' He pointed at the window. 'Those things are *our* growth-limiting factor. Maybe somehow Moreton found out that wasps are theirs.'

Giles stared at the window. Then, slowly, they both turned to look at the fireplace.

'I'll go,' said Giles.

There was a loud crack and one of the flies tore a strip of wood away from the window frame. As Joe backed away from the window, Giles knelt down and peered up the chimney.

'I think I can do it,' he said.

Joe shook his head. 'You'll never get up there. Your shoulders are too wide.'

'No they're not,' said Giles, sticking his head up the chimney and trying to wriggle his way in. But a few seconds later he backed out again, his face covered in soot. 'Yes they are,' he admitted.

'I'm smaller than you,' said Joe. 'Let me go.'

'But you *hate* wasps,' said Giles.

Joe pushed him out of the way. 'Maybe,' he said. 'But I hate those things even more.'

The entrance was narrow, but by hunching his shoulders he found he could wriggle his way up into the main chimney, which was slightly wider.

'How's it looking?' Giles called.

Joe looked up. Above him he could see a chink of light, but the top of the chimney was almost completely blocked by a large wasps' nest. As he stood with his feet in the fireplace he could hear the hum of a thousand wasps fanning their wings.

'Think you can make it?'

'Maybe.' Joe felt sick and his hands were shaking.

'Well, I don't want to hurry you,' Giles called nervously, 'but I think they're gonna be through any minute.'

Joe pressed his palms flat against the sides of the chimney and wedged his trainers against the brick-work.

'OK,' he said. 'I'm going.'

As he edged higher, the humming of wasps increased and he could see layers of wood pulp joined together in a large, cylindrical nest. Wasps flew in and out through a gap at the top of the chimney and Joe could see that the surface of the nest was crawling with them.

Tensing his arms against the brickwork he let out a long, slow breath.

Then, from below, he heard the crack of splinter-ing wood.

'You have to do something, Joe!' Giles shouted. 'You have to do something now!'

The fear in Giles's voice spurred Joe into action and he hurriedly scrabbled upward. As the wasps began to buzz around his head he gritted his teeth, drew back his fist and smashed it hard into the cen-tre of the nest.

His arm crunched through it like a ramrod, bursting out of the other side as the first hot needles of pain pierced his face and hands. As the wasps swarmed around him he shook his head from side to side, crying out in pain as they stung him viciously. But he kept moving higher, doggedly using his feet to push himself up. At last he reached the top and, with an angry shout, thrust his arm out through the chimney pot. As the nest disintegrated, rolling away across the roof tiles, the wasps renewed their attack with such ferocity that Joe felt as though his head was about to explode.

Unable to withstand the pain any longer, he took his hands away from the brickwork, hunched his shoulders and dropped like a stone, hitting the grate at the bottom with a bone-jarring crash. As he rolled coughing and spluttering into the bedroom, he saw that the carpet was covered in broken glass and three huge flies were crawling through a hole where the window used to be. Giles was backed into a corner, desperately throwing shards of glass at the insects as they advanced.

Half mad with pain, Joe ran across the room and kicked one of the insects so hard that it spun back through the window. As another flew down onto the carpet he swung a kick, lost his balance and hit the floor in a crunch of broken glass. The creature lunged at him but Giles grabbed his arm just in time, dragging him back as its powerful jaws stabbed at the spot where he had been lying only seconds before. As the two of them huddled together in the corner, Joe caught sight of his terrified reflection, mirrored a hundredfold in the fly's blood-red eyes. But as it scuttled forward and opened its jaws there was a hum from the chimney and a ribbon of yellow and black came twisting out of the fireplace, spreading like smoke across the room. Immediately, the fly's head began to swivel and twitch, its legs scraping frantically at its body as if it was trying to clean itself. Then with a buzzing of wings it fell sideways, spun around on its back and smashed into the wardrobe.

Joe lowered his hands and saw that the other flies were also on their backs now, twitching and buzzing as a swarm of angry wasps crawled over them. There was still a cloud of flies outside the window, but they too were starting to twitch and fall away.

'You were right,' breathed Giles. 'The wasps are attacking them.'

Then the window blew in and flies exploded across the walls in a splatter of orangey-red as the bed and wardrobe disintegrated in a storm of smoke and splintering wood. Joe threw himself on top of Giles just as the wall behind them blew apart, filling the air with dust and plaster. Coughing and rubbing his eyes, Joe heard a deep roar from the hallway and turned to see the door handle glowing red, wisps of smoke curling underneath the door. Then the door flew off its hinges and two black-clad figures wearing gas masks crashed into the room, one of them cradling a flame-thrower in his arms.

'Clear!' he shouted. There was a deafening clatter of rotor blades as a helicopter gunship swept past the house, searching for fresh targets. But before they could open up again with their heavy machine guns, the top of a ladder appeared outside the window, soon followed by another black-suited figure who hurriedly gave the pilots the all-clear. Joe looked out of the bedroom door and saw flames licking along the hallway. Then one of the men grabbed him roughly by the shoulders and dragged him across the room, bundling him into the arms of the man at the window who dumped him unceremoniously onto the ladder.

He scrambled down and fell exhausted onto the grass. Seconds later Giles landed next to him with a thump.

'Oh God,' he said as the bodies of giant flies curled up and burned all around them. 'Tell me it's over, Giles. Please tell me that it's all over.'

As he looked up, one of the black-clad figures

leaned over and took off his gas mask. Joe saw at once that it was Sergeant Harris.

'So,' said Harris, holding out his hand. 'How was your day?'

In spite of the pain, Joe managed a weak smile.

'I've had better,' he said.

And as he took the policeman's hand and pulled himself to his feet, he saw his father, walking through the smoke towards him.

39

It was turning out to be a good day for Milton Roberts. The antibiotics had kicked in and the infection in his shoulder wound had cleared up at last. He had been round collecting everyone's cups and made a list of library books so that everyone on the hospital ward could choose their favourites from the library trolley.

And it was still only ten-thirty in the morning.

'Milton Roberts,' said the ward sister, 'you're an absolute treasure. I really don't know what we're going to do without you.'

'Oh, I'm sure you'll manage,' Milton replied with a shy smile. But he was pleased nonetheless.

He was, of course, looking forward to getting back to the mortuary, assisting Doctor Page and giving everything a jolly good clean. But secretly – if the truth be told – a part of him was actually *glad* that those horrible creatures had attacked him. If they hadn't, well he would never have ended up here, would he? He would never have met all these lovely people. There was old Mrs Lewis at the end of the ward, always so friendly and cheerful despite her injuries. Then there was that softly spoken Mrs Barclay who was always so kind. Even Trevor, the bad-tempered plumber, had been grateful when Milton had showed him a book called *How to Make Money*.

'Soon as I'm back on my feet I'll be raking it in,' he'd said.

And Milton had smiled and said he was sure that he would.

Then, of course, there was the charming Mr Wilkinson who had suffered a mild heart attack after all the excitement. But it was obvious that a little thing like that wasn't going to slow him down for long. Milton liked Mr Wilkinson best of all, because he was Chair of the Parish Council and he understood how important it was for the world to be a neat, well-ordered place.

'So you're off then, Milton?' Mr Wilkinson asked as Milton folded up his pyjamas and packed them away in his overnight bag.

'Yes, Mr Wilkinson, I am,' said Milton. 'The doctors have given me a clean bill of health.'

'Well I must say, Milton, you've been a tonic for

us all. Sorting things out, getting us organised. It's been a pleasure to know you.'

For a moment Milton thought that he was going to cry. He had always thought of himself as someone who enjoyed working alone, but now he realised that this was simply the way his life had turned out. And suddenly, as he leaned forward and shook Mr Wilkinson's outstretched hand, it occurred to him just how much he was going to miss everybody.

'Are you alright, Milton?' asked Mr Wilkinson.

'Oh yes,' said Milton, wiping his eye with his sleeve. 'Just the bright sunshine, I expect.'

'Ah well,' said Mr Wilkinson. 'You take care of yourself now.'

'I will,' said Milton. 'Thank you very much.'

As he turned to walk away, Mr Wilkinson said, 'I'm sure that you must be extremely busy, what with your job and everything, but I don't suppose you would have any free time in the evenings at all?'

Milton stopped.

'I don't know. That is, I–'

'The reason I ask,' Mr Wilkinson went on, 'is that we have a vacancy on the Parish Council and I was just wondering if you might be interested. I mean, with your organisational skills and so on, you're exactly the kind of person the Parish Council needs.'

Milton watched the dust dancing in the sunlight.

'Me?' he asked. 'You want *me* on the Parish Council?'

'Of course,' said Mr Wilkinson. 'We'd love to have you. That is, if it wouldn't be too much trouble.'

'Oh no,' said Milton. 'It wouldn't be too much trouble at all.'

As he walked out of the door and along the corridor, Milton felt the burden of years falling away behind him.

People liked him.

He had finally found his place in this world.

And suddenly, as he walked across the car park with the sun on his face, Milton did something that he had never done before in his life. Breaking into a run, he leapt into the air, punched his fist into the sky and shouted:

'Yes! Yes! *Yes!*'

40

'He looks happy,' said Joe's dad as he eased the camper van into a free parking place.

The three of them watched the man run across the hospital car park, jumping and punching the air.

Joe smiled.

'Who'd have thought that hospitals could be so much fun?'

As Giles opened the van door Joe's dad said, 'We'll come with you if you like.'

'No, you're alright,' said Giles, climbing out into the car park. 'But thanks anyway. I won't be long.'

As they watched Giles walk through the hospital doors, Joe's dad asked, 'Is their house still in a mess?'

Joe nodded.

'The fire destroyed the hallway and part of the roof before they put it out.'

'Crikey. What will they do?'

'Oh, you know Giles. He's already got a building

firm round there. Sorted it through the insurance, apparently. And while they're working on it, he's made a bed up for his mum downstairs.'

'Even so. It can't be very nice for them.'

Joe shrugged.

'Beats being attacked by giant bugs, I s'pose.'

Joe's dad smiled.

'Well, yes. There is that.'

They were quiet for a while and Joe watched ragged wisps of cloud drift above the hospital.

'Dad,' he said. 'All this strange stuff that's been happening. Do you think it will change anything? About the way people treat the world, I mean.'

Joe's dad shook his head.

'I'm afraid not,' he said.

'Why?'

'Because, Joe, everyone thinks they've won, that's why. They think that because they've killed those things, everything's going to be alright.'

'And isn't it?'

'I don't know. Maybe. But you have to remember that, in a way, those creatures were fighting to protect the world. When we ventured so deep beneath the earth's surface, it was as though we somehow tapped into the planet's bloodstream. Those creatures simply reacted like the white blood cells do in our own bodies. To them we were just an infection that was spreading too far and too quickly. And once they had identified us, they did everything they could to kill us off. But although they were fighting against us, in a way they were fighting for us too. By trying to protect the world in which we live.'

Joe frowned.

'So they were a good thing, then?'

'Kind of. I sometimes wonder if those things we call bad can turn out to be good in the end. It's just that we can't always tell the difference between the two.'

'What do you mean?'

Joe's dad thought for a minute.

'Once, when you were little, you got a splinter in your finger. And your mum knew that if she left it in there, it would turn septic. So she heated up a needle to sterilise it, then sat you down on her lap, held you tight and dug the splinter out. You screamed the place down, I remember.'

He shook his head and smiled at the memory.

'Of course, you couldn't understand why your mum was hurting you, so you slapped her and ran upstairs to your bedroom. Then your mum cried too, because the last thing she had wanted to do was hurt you. But she knew she had to, because she didn't want the pain to get any worse.'

Joe stared out of the window, close to tears.

'I don't remember,' he said.

They were both silent for a while. Then Joe said, 'Mum dying was a bad thing, wasn't it?'

'Yes,' said his dad quietly. 'It was a very bad thing.'

'So how could it ever be a good thing too?'

For a moment Joe's dad didn't say anything. He chewed at a piece of dry skin at the edge of his thumbnail and stared at the clock on the dashboard.

'I'm sorry,' said Joe, suddenly feeling bad. 'I shouldn't have—'

'No, no, it's alright.' Joe's dad turned to face him. 'I don't know, Joe. I can't think of a single reason why your mum not being here could ever be a good thing. But the other day, I remembered something she said about fish.'

Joe shook his head. 'I don't understand,' he said.

'Oh, it was years ago now. When your mum and I were first going out together, we visited an aquarium. It was a freezing cold day, I remember, and we stayed there for ages, watching the fish. When we came out again, it had started snowing. And your mum said, "Those fish will never know, will they? They spend all their lives swimming about in their own little world, and they'll never know about the snow."'

Joe's dad gave a small, sad laugh.

'I thought it was funny at the time. But now,

whenever I think about it, it makes me think that perhaps the bad things in our lives are only a small part of a much bigger picture. Maybe there's a whole lot of snow out there that we just don't know about.'

As Joe watched Giles and Mrs Barclay walking towards them across the car park, he imagined snow falling softly outside an aquarium. He thought of his mother, years ago, hurting him in order to make him better.

And as his father put an arm around his shoulders he wondered if maybe the world kept its secrets for a reason; that maybe not knowing all of them wasn't such a bad thing after all.

41

'You really shouldn't have come all this way to pick me up,' said Giles's mother as she settled into the back seat next to Giles. 'I could easily have got a taxi.'

'It's no problem,' said Joe's dad. He smiled. 'In fact, it's a pleasure.'

He turned the key in the ignition and the engine made a *wuh-wuh-wuh-wuh* sound.

'Oh, come on now,' he said, patting the dashboard by way of encouragement. 'Don't start playing up on me today.'

He turned the key again.

Wuh-wuh-wuh-wuh went the engine.

Joe's dad raised his eyes skywards, waited a few seconds, then turned the key a third time.

This time, the engine just went *click*.

'Oh great,' he said. 'That's all we need.'

'Did it start OK this morning?' asked Giles's mum.

'Yes, fine. I don't know–'

'Maybe it's your distributor cap or something. Do you want me to take a look at it?'

'I, well, if–'

'Won't be a tick,' said Giles's mum. She jumped out of the van and seconds later she had disappeared beneath the bonnet.

'Don't worry,' said Giles, seeing the look of confusion on Joe's dad's face. 'She knows what she's doing.'

A minute later Giles's mum reappeared, wiping her hands on the front of her jeans.

'Try it now.'

Joe watched her through the windscreen and, as she wiped a smudge of oil from her forehead, he was surprised at how much younger she looked. Maybe, he thought, it had something to do with the fact that she was smiling. And as the engine burst into life, her smile grew wider and then suddenly they were all laughing and cheering, and it felt like a new beginning.

On the journey home Joe's dad was more animated than Joe had seen him in a long time. He talked about the waves they would catch and the barbecues they would cook when they finally got down to the coast.

'I'll tell you something,' he said, 'this holiday has been a long time coming.'

When they pulled up outside Giles's house, Joe saw the black scorch marks on the front wall and a huge piece of plastic sheeting over the roof, flapping in the breeze.

'Home sweet home,' said Giles's mum, and Joe noticed that she was no longer smiling.

But as she opened the door of the van, Joe's dad said, 'You could come with us, you know. If you want to.'

Giles's mum stepped out onto the pavement and looked at the builders' vans in the driveway. Then she looked back at the camper van.

'Oh no,' she said. 'We couldn't possibly. There's hardly enough room for the two of you as it is.'

Joe's dad shrugged.

'Who cares? We've got an old tent back at home. We could easily stop off and get that.' He leaned out of the window and added in a low whisper, 'I wouldn't normally ask. But to be honest, I think I'm going to need a mechanic.'

Joe looked at Giles's mum and saw that she was smiling again, and so was Giles.

'Come on,' said Joe's dad. 'What do you say?'

'Alright,' she said. 'Give us ten minutes.'

* * *

245

Late that afternoon, when the camper van reached the top of the last hill, Joe thought of all the strange things that had happened. He thought of the nights he had lain awake, believing that the end of the road was just around the corner.

But they were still travelling, weren't they?

They were still moving forward, with the sun on their faces and the wind in their hair.

He looked at Giles, deep in thought, remembering how he had talked of being lifted above the sand between his mother and father.

Of how it had felt like flying.

He thought of his own mother then, running towards the waves all those years ago.

Through the open window, the ocean sparkled silver in the distance.

'You know what, Giles?' he said. 'I think we made it.'

Giles smiled.

Then he clenched his fist and bumped his knuckles against Joe's.

'You know what?' he said. 'I think we did.'

As the camper van began its slow descent toward the sea, Joe thought, *Tomorrow we shall swim like fish.*

He imagined himself in the cool of the ocean, moving through the shadows and into the light while all around him the world kept on spinning its secrets; secrets that would remain forever hidden in the sea and the snow and the sunlight and stars.